ABOUT THE AUTHOR

Handsome, young and talented, Jason Herbison doesn't just write about soap, he lives it! Jason works as a full-time television scriptwriter and is the Australian correspondent for the magazine, *Inside Soap*.

Jason began writing for television at eighteen, securing a regular position on the story team of *Neighbours*. He has also worked on *Paradise Beach*, *Shortland Street*, *Home & Away*, *Echo Point* and *Pacific Drive*. As well as working for television, Jason has written and produced a short film called *The Dive*. Jason lives in Sydney.

THE BIG BREAK

JASON HERBISON

Hodder
Children's
Books

a division of Hodder Headline Limited

This edition of *The Big Break* and *The Price of Fame*
first published as a single volume in 2000.

ISBN 0 340 80522 6

10 9 8 7 6 5 4 3 2 1

For Mum and Dad

The Big Break

First published as a single volume in Australia in 1996
by Hodder Headline Australia Pty Limited
(A member of the Hodder Headline Group)

First published as a single volume in Great Britain in 1997
by Hodder Children's Books

A Catalogue record for this book
is available from the British Library

Typeset by Hewer Text Ltd, Edinburgh
Printed and bound in Great Britain by
Clays Ltd, St Ives plc

Hodder Children's Books
a division of Hodder Headline Limited
338 Euston Road
London NW1 3BH

PART ONE

CHAPTER ONE

BONDI PLACE

AUDITION SCENE:

SCENE 10.   **INT. SURF CAFE**   **AFTERNOON**

STEFAN, RACINE, EMILY, *N/S EXTRAS

THE CAFE IS QUIET. STEFAN IS PREPARING SANDWICHES BEHIND THE COUNTER, WHILE RACINE FLICKS THROUGH THE PAGES OF A FASHION MAGAZINE.

RACINE
These clothes are so boring! Even I could do better with a needle and thread.

STEFAN
That'll be the day. Stick to your credit card.

EMILY ENTERS. SHE TENTATIVELY APPROACHES THE COUNTER.

STEFAN
(TO EMILY) G'day. What can I get for you?

EMILY
I'm here about the job advertised in the window. Part-time waitress?

RACINE
Then you need to talk to me. My father owns this cafe. In fact, he owns just about everything on this beach.

STEFAN
(ANNOYED) And he left me in charge of interviewing applicants. What's your name?

EMILY
Emily.

RACINE
Pay no attention to him! The salt water's affected his brain. Now, what experience do you have?

EMILY
I've been working in a petrol station for six months.

RACINE ROLLS HER EYES.

RACINE
We don't get many cars in here.

EMILY
(EMBARRASSED) I'm sorry. I mean . . . I've been working in the restaurant section. I can do everything — cook, clean . . .

BY THIS TIME STEFAN HAS BACKED OUT OF THE CONVER-SATION AND IS LOOKING OUT THE WINDOW. HE DOESN'T LIKE WHAT HE SEES.

STEFAN
Panic stations! A tidal wave of tourists are heading this way. (TO RACINE) You're going to have to pitch in and help.

RACINE
I'm busy!

STEFAN
Thought you'd say that. (TO EMILY) Job's yours. Hope you weren't in a hurry.

STEFAN TOSSES AN APRON TO EMILY, MUCH TO RACINE'S IRRITATION.

FREEZE FRAME ON EMILY, NERVOUS BUT EXCITED TO HAVE THE JOB.

* NON-SPEAKING

Jessica had read the scene a hundred times, considered every emotional angle and perfected a powerhouse performance. Yes, she knew exactly how to play the character of Racine. At least, she hoped she did.

The taxi screeched to a halt in the East Sydney street directly in front of Carter Castings. The building was impossible to miss: offensive orange-painted walls, dark windows and a palm tree adding a 'Hollywood' feel. Jessica decided it looked more like a manufacturing plant than the breeding ground for the stars of tomorrow. She tipped the driver a couple of dollars, hoping this act of generosity would be returned to her in the form of the big break she'd been dreaming about. Then again, she wasn't too sure about that either.

Taking a deep breath, she adjusted her vibrant red hair and pushed through the rotating glass doors. *This is it*, she reminded herself. *There's no turning back now*.

All but one of the twelve seats in the reception area were occupied by potential 'Racines'. Some looked nervous, others confident, the remainder struggling somewhere in between. The stark blue walls featured portraits of all the famous names who had passed through. Unlike her peers, Jessica never had imagined her face amongst them. Fame and fortune held no appeal; she simply wanted to act. This made her feel guilty enough.

All eyes checked her out as she approached the circular reception desk. Every new arrival spelt competition. Jessica was an enemy. Fortunately, the young male receptionist greeted her with a cheerful smile.

"You must be Jessica Fairgate," he said, in between bites of a chocolate bar.

"Good guess," she replied.

"Not really," he explained as he revealed the large black and white photograph forwarded by her agent. "You're the last Racine on our list. Shouldn't be too long."

"Thanks."

She turned around to discover the other girls looking her up and down. Her mind filled with an image of a crocodile pit – gaping jaws eager to chop her into pieces. Snapping back to reality, the first thing she noticed was how undressed to impress they were – high cut minis, sexy bustiers and exposed midriffs. They obviously saw the character of Racine as a down-market vamp, more King's Cross than Double Bay. Jessica immediately regretted spending so much money on her junior executive look. A smart olive jacket with a matching pleated skirt seemed a suitable purchase at the time. Now she was having second thoughts.

She settled into the only remaining chair and prepared for the longest wait of her life. Time was the last thing she needed: time to actually think about what she was doing, time to consider what was really at stake. This was survival of the fittest. One part talent, three parts determination. The more she thought about it, the more she lacked in the second department. Suddenly her knees turned to jelly and her head began to spin. *What am I doing here?* she asked herself. *What am I trying to achieve?*

The question was much too stressful to contemplate. She reached over to the side table and picked up a copy of *Woman's World*, hoping a few pages of idle gossip would help her relax. Instead, a different type of headline caught her attention. 'TEENAGE DECEPTION – EVERY PARENT'S NIGHTMARE!' A middle-aged couple, who bore a chilling resemblance to her own parents, were pictured inside a house while a teenager – presumably their son – was pictured stealing a car. The message: parents have no idea what their kids are up to. Jessica related to this all too well. At that very moment her parents believed she was talking to her school careers adviser about Year Eleven electives. They had no idea she was in hot pursuit of an acting career which, if successful, would require her to abandon her studies, at least on a full-time basis. The Fairgates valued education above all else. Jessica was expected to complete high school and then attend university. A law degree and a stable career would naturally follow. Anything else was akin to a life of crime.

Jessica's head followed the logic. The statistics on unemployed actors were alarming – less than ten percent actually working. She didn't want to end up waiting tables but the alternatives – such as working in a law firm – were even less appealing. Her heart craved excitement. *So what if only ten percent of actors are working?* she told herself. *I can be in that ten percent.* Ever since she played the lead in her school production of *Summer of the Seventeenth Doll*, a passion to

perform had consumed her. Sometimes it felt like a
calling, although this sounded far too corny to admit.
The question she had dismissed moments earlier as too
hard was answered. *What am I doing here? I'm following my heart*, she concluded. She also knew anything
involving her heart was dangerous.

"Hi," said a voice from beside her.

Jessica looked over and vaguely recognised the
smiling face above the impressive cleavage. The girl
looked like a tart – tacky gold earrings, a tight pink
dress and black stilettos.

"You're Jessica, aren't you?" she said.

Jessica nodded.

"I'm Samantha Murdoch. We met at the toothpaste
commercial last week."

Now Jessica remembered. They had both auditioned for non-speaking roles but lost to stick-figure
supermodel types. The rejection had left Jessica with a
complex about her weight for days.

"Oh, hi. Nice to see you again," she replied.

"Are you going for the part of Racine?" Samantha
enquired.

"Absolutely. And you?"

"Of course. I wouldn't have put this colour through my hair if I wasn't." Samantha parted her golden locks, illustrating why Jessica had failed to recognise her – the last time they met, Samantha had been a brunette. "You're taking a bit of a risk staying as a redhead, aren't you?" she continued.

Jessica was confused. "Why would I change my hair colour?"

"I figured you knew," Samantha explained. "They want Racine to be a bottle-blonde. My agent said I had to bleach if I really wanted to win the role."

Jessica looked around the room. Sure enough, all the other girls were survivors of a peroxide explosion. *How could my agent forget to tell me?* she cursed silently. But looking at Samantha's satisfied expression, she began to doubt whether what she had said was actually true. She didn't trust Samantha. Her mind flashed back to the crocodiles. *Maybe she's trying to set me up? Trying to pressure me into walking out?*

Jessica was smart enough to know she could react in either of two ways – allow the information to undermine her confidence, or use it to her advantage.

"At least they'll have no trouble remembering me," she replied, successfully turning the negative into a positive. Even if Samantha's tip was false it had given her the extra shot of motivation she needed – she always performed better when the odds were stacked against her.

"Good luck anyway," cooed Samantha as she reached into her purse and produced a small compact to touch up her make-up. Very much the picture of Racine. Cool and calculating. Jessica had to admit this girl would be hard to beat.

Looking back at the magazine, she flipped back a few pages and landed on another article: 'FOLLOW YOUR DREAMS.' She considered this a good omen. *I'll follow my heart and my head will sort out the rest*, she decided. *That sounds like a good plan.*

* * *

"Job's yours. Hope you weren't in a hurry." Blake flicked his dark brown hair back to reveal deep brown eyes which smiled for the camera. This smile could melt a thousand hearts. And he knew it.

"Cut," said Diana Carter, a former actress in her late fifties who was now one of Australia's most influential casting directors. An attractive woman beneath a tough exterior, she wore red-rimmed glasses and her charcoal hair in a rigid bun. Blake thought she resembled one of his least favourite primary school teachers.

"How did I do?" he asked.

"Okay," she replied.

Blake nearly burst a blood vessel. He wanted to hear he was incredible, even superb. Diana was half-convinced. There was no doubt Blake had the physical requirements for surfer Stefan – tousled hair, tanned skin and muscular physique. What she was uncertain about could be satisfied in either of two ways. Ideally, Blake had to be a good actor to play the emotions required. Or, his own personality needed to be similar enough to Stefan's in order to make the performance credible on screen. Diana suspected the latter.

"On second thoughts, keep rolling," she instructed her assistant, who was actually a work experience student finding the job far less exciting than he had anticipated. A dimly-lit room and a dodgy, hand-held

camera pointed at a chair was hardly a glamorous
setting. Under these circumstances, Blake had to pretend he was in a trendy Bondi Beach cafe, a difficult
task for even the most talented of actors. He had
dressed in a fluorescent shirt and board shorts to help
him capture the vibe, but it wasn't working. To make
matters worse, the only window overlooked an overflowing rubbish bin.

"So, how much time did you spend on this?" Diana
asked in a dubious tone.

Blake found it difficult to speak. He couldn't stop
seeing his teacher and remembering the way she used
to interrogate him about his homework. He was
terrified of her.

"Three days," he finally replied, making a conscious
effort to put images of his school years behind him.
"Even passed up a shopping mall parade to be here. If
you don't believe me you can ask my agent!"

Diana didn't doubt it for a minute. Blake's scrapbook was resting on her lap and it was overflowing
with cuttings of him modelling clothes in department
store catalogues and photographs taken on the catwalk. She knew he was hot property.

"Tell me what you think Stefan's story is," she continued.

Blake was momentarily thrown. He was not much good at these kinds of questions – utterly hopeless when it came to expressing anything in words unless he was reading it off a page. Fortunately, he had an excellent memory and recalled something Mel Gibson had said in an interview.

"Well, I think Stefan is extremely complex and three-dimensional. He is on an emotional journey."

Diana suspected this was a borrowed comeback but found it quite endearing. The character of Stefan was also a smooth talker, the kind of guy who could copy an essay and have the original author charged with the rip-off. He was a bit of a con artist and Diana recognised a similar trait in Blake.

"Fair enough. Now tell me a little more about yourself," she continued, glancing over the question-naire he'd filled out a few moments earlier. "I see you've just turned sixteen. You've been modelling part time for three years and now you want to act. Why?"

Blake knew he had to answer very carefully. The yellow brick road from modelling to acting was well yet rarely successfully walked, especially by people his age. For once in his life, honesty seemed like the best policy.

"I sort of fell into modelling. But acting is what I want to do. I took a few lessons and decided it was the way to go. I guess I was always the class clown and acting is a way to make money out of it."

"What about finishing school?"

"What about it?"

"If – and I mean if – we offered you the role of Stefan, we would naturally provide a tutor for you to continue your studies part-time. Do you think you could cope with the workload?"

Blake stared intently into the camera, as if facing the barrel of a loaded gun and matching it with equal fire. "School is good for some but not for me. I want to be an actor. And I want to give it one hundred percent."

Diana smiled for the first time since the audition began. The character of Stefan had a similar attitude to education and it was a big advantage that Blake shared this. Lastly, the part of the job she loved and loathed. There was a fine line when it came to exploitation in the industry and casting directors are well aware that they teeter on the threshold. Now more relaxed, Blake had absolutely no hesitation stripping his shirt off to parade for the camera.

"And you don't mind frolicking around the beach in a pair of Speedos?" she asked.

"Do it all the time," Blake assured her.

"Thank you very much," she said, gesturing at him to put his shirt back on. "Don't go skipping the country."

Blake interpreted this as a good sign.

* * *

Holly burst through the doors of Carter Castings, out of breath and an hour late for her audition. The receptionist was busy deadlocking the windows.

"Excuse me," Holly panted, adjusting the scrunchy in her long blonde hair and tucking her wayward green shirt into her jeans. "I'm Holly Harrison. I was supposed to be here at five but the bus broke down and I couldn't get to a phone."

None of this made much sense to the receptionist. "I'm sorry, but the auditions have finished. You were the last for the day and Diana couldn't wait. If you'd phoned . . ."

"But I told you, I couldn't," Holly protested as if her life depended on it.

"I truly am sorry. There's nothing I can do. Diana is presenting the tapes to the producer tonight, so we can't even reschedule you for tomorrow."

Holly felt like her entire world was crashing around her. After the trouble she'd gone to in making her way to Sydney. A bus from Ballina at seven in the morning, followed by a long journey sitting next to a blabber-mouth man with bad breath. Not to mention the effort and expense involved in finding out about the audition in the first place! The thought of returning home a failure practically reduced her to tears. It was then Diana returned, all a fluster.

"Damn it! I forgot the Polaroids! Karen will have a fit if I turn up without the Polaroids!" she complained as she backtracked to her office.

Diana was referring to Karen Wolfe, producer of *Bondi Place*. The two women were to watch the audition tapes later in the evening and narrow down the best of the actors for presentation to the executives at Channel Eleven the next day. Although the final casting decisions rested with the network, Diana and Karen were very good at pushing their favourites.

Holly knew this was her second chance and she wasn't about to let it slip away. Before the receptionist could argue, Holly was hot on her heels.

"Miss Carter," she called out. Diana paused. "I'm Holly Harrison. I've just been speaking to your receptionist. There's been a terrible misunderstanding with my audition time." She lowered her voice. "You see, he told me six pm and apparently you had me down for five. I'd really appreciate it if you could audition me now."

Holly was amazed how easily the lie rolled off her tongue. She didn't want to get the receptionist into trouble, nor did she want to risk getting caught out herself, but somehow she said it and somehow it sounded convincing. Ordinarily Diana would have said 'Bad luck', but she saw a sparkle of star quality in Holly which prompted her to make an exception.

"I don't remember seeing your photo," said Diana. "Who is your agent?"

Now Holly had to spin another lie. The truth was

she didn't actually have an acting agent but had made appointments to see several the following day.

"I'm with the Shooting Star Agency. I asked them not to forward my photo as I've just had some new ones taken."

Holly reached into her bag and produced several black and white photographs of herself, ranging from happy to sad to mad expressions. She had spent all her savings paying a professional photographer to take them. Diana was impressed, though her face gave nothing away.

"You're auditioning for the part of Racine?" Diana asked.

"No – Emily," Holly corrected her. "I'm very much in tune with her. We're both from the country. I even did work experience in a petrol station!"

Diana softened ever so slightly. There was something appealing about Holly, although she couldn't put her finger on it. Those in the industry referred to this as the 'X' factor.

"Okay. The work experience kid has gone for the day so I'll audition you on my own. We'll have to be quick."

Holly heaved a huge sigh of relief. Her devastation had turned into delight in just a few seconds.

"Just one thing," Diana added. "Since we don't have much time, forget Emily – I want you to audition for a different part. I'll give you a couple of minutes to learn the new scene."

Holly was gobsmacked. *Someone else? After all the work I've done on Emily!* she thought.

Before Holly knew what was happening, Diana took her picture with the Polaroid camera and 1handed her three pages of lines to learn. Slumping into a chair, Holly thought of her friends back at home and how she'd soon be sitting in the classroom with them again, moaning about her adventure to the city and how badly she'd stuffed up. Having lost the chance to read for Emily, and with only a few minutes to learn another role, she felt certain she could kiss her dream goodbye.

CHAPTER TWO

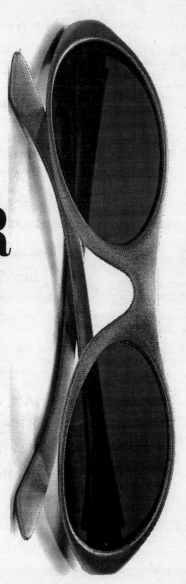

ACTOR'S AGREEMENT
for
BONDI PLACE

The Parties to this agreement are

a) Actor: JESSICA BETH FAIRGATE
    Address: c/o ANDERSON ACTORS
                AGENCY
                299 Mint Street
                Double Bay
                Sydney 2011

                            (The "Actor")

b) Producer: CHANNEL ELEVEN DRAMA
                UNIT PTY. LTD.
                12–24 Hogan Street
                North Bondi 2060

                            (The "Producer")

Meredith Fairgate held the document in her hands. She was completely mystified. *What did any of this have to do with her Jessica? It couldn't possibly be an authentic contract, could it?*

Meredith watched as Jessica performed pirouettes on the lower balcony of their spectacular three-level home which overlooked the famous Sydney Harbour Bridge and Opera House. A boat, full of Japanese tourists, had just appeared in the cove and Jessica was having a great time entertaining them. This was what she loved most about living on the water – pulling really crazy stunts when the boats sailed past.

Jessica spun around and almost bumped into her mother. From a distance they could have been twins. They were the same height, walked alike and shared the dual curse and blessing of red hair. Jessica's laughter faded quickly when she noticed the contract in her mother's hand.

"You've been in my room," she accused.

"What is all this about?" asked Meredith.

Jessica took a deep breath. "I only found out this morning. I've been trying to think of a way to tell you."

"I can see that," Meredith managed to reply. "I suppose that's why you've been making phone calls to your friends all day. They must know more about this than we do."

Meredith's face portrayed hurt more than anger. She prided herself on having an open and honest relationship with Jessica and was saddened to realise this was not totally true.

Jessica felt terribly guilty. There was a lot she hadn't told her parents. She knew they would be concerned about her studies and wanted to spend at least one day celebrating before she braved the explanation scene. Unfortunately, the music had stopped earlier than she expected.

"You know how I've always wanted to be an actress," she began, her voice quivering with nerves and trepidation.

"Is that before or after you wanted to be a marine biologist?" Meredith wondered in a slightly sarcastic tone.

Jessica conceded that this was a fair point. "Okay, so I've changed my mind a few times. But now I'm certain that I want to act and this is the big break I've been waiting for. It's a new show called *Bondi Place*. I've been offered a leading role."

Jessica searched her mother's face for some sign of pride or approval, but all she found was bewilderment. She figured she'd better do some more explaining. "As for my studies, the agency has negotiated a tutor so I'll be able to continue Year Eleven part-time."

"The agency?" said Meredith incredulously.

"Guess I forgot to tell you about that as well," Jessica explained weakly, knowing full well she'd worked very hard to keep it a secret. "I registered with an acting agency a few weeks ago."

"Why didn't you tell us any of this? You've never had to keep secrets from us in the past."

"I was worried about your reaction. I know how much you want me to concentrate on school and go on to uni."

The look of uncertainty on her mother's face confirmed that Jessica had good reason to worry. With no other option, she decided to play her trump card. "Remember how you always wanted to be an opera singer, but you didn't pursue it and have regretted it ever since?" she asked.

Meredith recalled telling Jessica this story a few years ago.

"Well, *I* don't want to have any regrets."

Meredith paused for what seemed like an eternity. She genuinely wanted what was best for Jessica and believed education was essential. However, she didn't want to sound like a hypocrite. "I guess . . . I guess I'd better start watching television."

A wave of relief washed over Jessica and she gave her mother a hug. Moments later, a thought unnerved her again. "What about . . .?"

"Don't worry – I'll talk to your father."

Jessica smiled and returned to the comfort of her mother's arms. Out on the harbour another boat-load of tourists appeared and applauded. Jessica considered it a premonition. Soon the entire nation would be watching her. Hopefully, they too would be cheering.

*　*　*

The country air was soft and warm, the sky a brilliant blue. Holly had finished her homework, which meant the rest of the day was her own. Unfortunately, this

equalled perfect conditions for dreaming and she had
made a solemn vow never to do that again.

The subjects of television, stardom and *Bondi Place*
had been banned on the Harrison farm since Holly
returned from Sydney two weeks earlier. She was
convinced she had no hope of winning the role of
Racine which Diana had asked her to read. She
thought her pony 'Zac' – renowned for his laziness
but named after her favourite television star Zac
Winter – would win the Melbourne Cup before that
happened.

Her father Bill was on horseback, busy rounding up
sheep in a nearby paddock. A grey-haired man in his
late fifties, Bill was often mistaken for Holly's grand-
father and had a rare, rugged quality about him.
Suddenly Bill's mobile phone rang and he reached
into his pocket to answer it.

Bill asked the caller to repeat himself three times
before galloping over and handing the phone to Holly.
"For you. Some fella named Darren Bennett."

Holly's heart skipped a beat. Darren managed the
Shooting Star Agency. She had listed them as her
agent when she auditioned for *Bondi Place* but, when

she dropped in after her audition seeking representation, Darren scolded her for her dishonesty and told her never to darken his door again. *What's he doing calling me now?* she wondered.

"Hello?" she said.

"Hi kid. Good to talk to you again. Fantastic news."

Holly was taken aback. *Fantastic news?*

"You've got the gig on *Bondi P*. Contract's here on my desk. Six months with an option."

Holly couldn't believe her ears. She had so thoroughly convinced herself all was lost that this seemed like a cruel prank the immature boys at Ballina High would play. However, she distinctly recognised Darren's slimy tone. "Are you for real? I've got the part of Racine?"

"You betcha. Be here at ten tomorrow morning. We've got a lot to talk about. You can't do the show without an agent to look after you."

In reality Darren was looking after Darren. As Holly's agent, he would take ten percent of her weekly earnings which amounted to a major profit for very little work. Holly had read thousands of books on the entertainment industry and was well aware of his vested interest. This was all too much for her to consider. At the realisation of all her dreams, her abject disappointment was turning into jubilation. But she couldn't forget how badly Darren had treated her when she attempted to join his agency.

"But you told me never to darken your door again," she reminded him.

"Look up in the sky," Darren responded. "The sun is shining on you again. See you tomorrow."

The mobile promptly cut out. Holly looked up to the sky where indeed the sun was in full force. She slowly began to realise the implications of the phone call. *I'm going to be a star!* she mused. *I've made it*!

Three seconds later she let fly an enormous 'Yippee!' Looking over to Zac, she thought of all the hours she'd spent riding him, dreaming about life as a television star and the day she might meet his namesake. The dream was about to become a reality. Soon she would be working at Channel Eleven – home of the real Zac Winter.

* * *

"So how much are they gonna pay you?" asked Eddie Dexter in between slurps of warm beer. An overweight man in his late thirties, he'd smoked far too many cigarettes and concluded every sentence with a mild cough. He claimed the beer soothed his throat.

"More than I get for wearing dodgy clothes on a catwalk," replied Blake, as he attempted to find carpet underneath the trail of pizza cartons, dirty laundry and assorted clutter which littered the living room floor. "I'm sure I put my contract here somewhere."

Blake stood up and surveyed the bomb site which he and his father called home. A jumbo jet thundered overhead, causing the walls to shake and the television reception to crackle. This happened every few minutes, the consequence of life under the flight path. It was then that Blake noticed a folded document beneath the leg of the television set, keeping it balanced. "Dad!" he bellowed as he kneeled down to retrieve his contract.

"I stuffed that there for a reason," said Eddie. "Now look what you've done!"

Blake didn't care that the television set was once again unstable. All he cared about was his contract, now stained with food and beer. He opened his mouth to blast his father but thought better of it. No matter how much he argued or how loud he shouted, Eddie wasn't going to change and Blake had learned to live with it. After all, he loved his father and knew Eddie loved him. A call to his agent and the contract could be replaced.

"So what's the dirt on this show, um, Bondi Beach?" Eddie asked as if the heated moment had never happened.

"I told you last night," said Blake.

Eddie thought back over the night before and screwed up his face, much like a little child who has been caught with his hand in the cookie jar. "Oh, right. Had a few drinks with the boys, didn't I?"

"I never would have guessed," said Blake sarcastically.

"You'd better tell me again," Eddie suggested.

"It's called *Bondi Place*. It's going to be filmed around Campbell Parade, you know, the main drag down at Bondi. I'm playing this character called Stefan. He's a lifesaver."

"Sounds like lots of babes in bikinis."

Blake flashed his devilish smile. "S'pose there might be one or two."

"Reckon you could get your old man a job? I'm pretty good at rubbing in sunscreen."

Blake laughed. "I'd better head down to the agency and see about that contract."

"Put in a good word for me!" Eddie added.

Blake paused at the front door. There was a subject he had to broach with his father and he wasn't sure how it would be received. Now the mood had brightened he decided to get it over and done with.

"Um . . . Dad. About school – I'm dropping out, okay?"

Eddie considered this for a moment. He genuinely cared about his son and having missed out on an education himself he regarded school as important. However, he also believed Blake had talent and it was wise to let him pursue it.

"On one condition," he began. "That is, if this show – *Bondi* whatever – doesn't work out, you'll go back. Have we got a deal?"

"Deal!"

Blake continued on his way, relieved that his father

had seen things his way. That's what he liked most about Eddie. He may have been a slob who drank too much, but he was always supportive. As for the condition, Blake felt certain *Bondi Place* was his ticket to the good life. School was already a bad memory.

CHAPTER
THREE

CHANNEL **11** ELEVEN
12–24 HOGAN ROAD   NORTH BONDI   SYDNEY

TO: ALL CAST AND CREW
FROM: KAREN WOLFE
CC: SIR ANGUS BEAZEL
          BOARD OF DIRECTORS
RE: *BONDI PLACE*

Congratulations and welcome to Bondi Place!

I have worked in the Australian television industry for over twenty years on numerous productions but never in my experience have I been so excited about a project. Bondi Place has the potential to become a local and international success and I'm sure you share my enthusiasm and dedication. There's a lot of hard work ahead but there's also a lot of fun!

I invite you to a cast and crew barbecue at Bondi Surf Life Saving Club next Saturday afternoon. The club is our most important location for the series so I feel it is an appropriate setting to get to know each other before production commences. For the less experienced members of the cast, it will be an environment in which to ask us veterans anything you may be concerned about!

I'm sure you're all very eager to know more about the show and I can assure you there is a lot of reading on the way -- over the next couple of days you'll be receiving comprehensive outlines and scripts for the first week of episodes.

Congratulations again and I look forward to seeing you on the weekend.

Karen Wolfe

Karen Wolfe
Producer

The sun cast brilliant rays of golden light over Bondi Beach. The famous stretch of sand was crowded as always. At the north end the musclemen reigned supreme, their golden suntans on display for all to ogle and admire. Several games of volleyball were in progress, though the players seemed more interested in watching the people watching them than actually concentrating on the ball. The middle of the beach was teeming with families of all ages and nationalities, each stamping their precious plot of sand with distinctive towels and umbrellas. Surfers seemed to have control of the south end, regularly taking time out from the waves to scoff a bucket of hot chips or a chicko roll.

The Bondi Surf Life Saving Club was a striking part of the spectacular surf and carnival atmosphere. On this afternoon the upper balcony was a hive of activity. Waiters undressed to imitate lifesavers carried trays of drinks, a band warbled a set of surf classics, and a barbecue banquet sizzled.

"I've really hit the big time," said Holly as she surveyed the action from the passenger seat of her father's utility truck parked on Campbell Parade, the cafe-crazed street where the fictional residents of *Bondi Place* would live. She was both nervous and excited about the afternoon ahead of her.

"But you're still my little girl," Bill replied.

"How do I look?" Holly demanded.

Bill's heart skipped a beat. He felt a mixture of sadness and pride. Holly was wearing a cream cable-knit dress which she had painstakingly made herself, the design copied from a dress modelled by Elle MacPherson in a magazine.

"Just like your mother. I wish she was here today."

Holly smiled. She, too, wished her mother could share her happiness. But that was impossible and life must go on. And for Holly, life was progressing at full speed.

"Say 'hi' to Auntie Agro for me. Tell her I'm really looking forward to living with her," she said in a tone which suggested quite the opposite.

Auntie Agro was Holly's Auntie Agnes. She lived on the outskirts of Sydney and Holly hated visiting her. However, not knowing another soul in the harbour city, Auntie Agnes was her only option for a place to live while working on *Bondi Place*.

"Don't forget to ask that producer woman about a tutor. Your studies are still the most important thing," Bill insisted, very much the concerned and protective father. Holly nodded, but in reality school had plummeted to the bottom of her priorities.

"Pick you up at seven?"

"Thanks Dad."

Holly gave her father a kiss before jumping out of the ute. A few seconds later she disappeared in the direction of the surf club. Bill didn't realise it at the time, but his little girl would never be the same again.

* * *

Karen Wolfe stood at the bottom of the steps, heading a stretch of red carpet which covered the footpath all the way up to Campbell Parade. An immaculately presented woman who looked much younger than her forty-two years, she seemed less concerned about her guests than about curious passers-by kicking sand on the carpet.

"This is a private party," she exclaimed as a potbellied man and his wife approached. "And I don't remember hiring either of you!"

The couple took offence and backed away, even though Karen didn't mean them any harm. She was simply a nervous producer with a lot of network executives to please, not to mention a cast and crew who were yet to meet each other. She smiled as a familiar face approached.

"Geraldo!" she beamed. Although it was the middle of the day, the crowd of turning heads indicated a brilliant star was shining. Geraldo Mercardo was a Greek Australian in his late forties and the biggest name signed to *Bondi Place*. At almost six feet tall, he was unmistakable. Of more interest was the leggy blonde clinging to his arm. Several photographers leapt to attention and began taking photos.

"Hello darling!" he said to Karen. "I do hope the champagne is on ice."

"Who's the girl?" asked one of the photographers, as if the young lady was just a new and tasty piece of meat.

"This is my fiancée, Ulrika Walstrom," Geraldo explained, putting his arm around her and smiling for the cameras. Karen shared the photographers' excitement – this startling development would surely make the papers and provide excellent publicity for the show.

"What's the story? Where did you meet?" asked another as he produced a pen and paper from his pocket.

"Are you Swedish?" asked another.

"Norwegian," she replied.

"That's all we can say," Geraldo explained. In other words they had sold their story as an exclusive to a magazine and were obliged to keep the details a secret.

The couple proceeded inside. A couple of minutes later the next star appeared, but this time the photographers showed no interest.

"Hi Karen," said Holly, doing her best to cover her nervousness. "You sure know how to throw a party!"

Karen welcomed Holly with an affectionate hug. Ever since she saw her wide blue eyes radiating on the audition tape, Karen knew Holly had star quality. In many ways, she felt quite maternal toward her. Never married and childless herself, Karen compensated by taking newcomers like Holly under her wing. It was hard to believe they'd only met a few days earlier in Darren Bennett's office at the Shooting Star Agency.

"I'm glad you could make it. Is your father here?"

Holly felt the twinge of her guilty conscience. She had not actually invited him to accompany her, fearing he would bore everyone with talk of wool prices and drought damage to crops. "He couldn't make it. Family business to attend to," she said convincingly.

"There's someone I think you should meet," said Karen, whisking Holly into the club.

Holly's adrenalin pumped into overdrive. *Is that really Geraldo Mercardo up ahead?* she wondered. *What will I say when I meet him?*

* * *

Jessica and Holly had been talking non-stop for ten minutes, having been introduced by Karen and left to get to know each other. Holly was still a little disappointed at not meeting Geraldo, though she figured star introductions would follow sooner or later. Just to be sure, she sat facing the crowd and smiled, reserving extra sparkle for the occasional famous face. Jessica kept her back to the action and was barely identifiable under a wide-brimmed sunhat, protecting her from her natural enemy – the sun. Put a stamp on them and you'd have a postcard of two very different girls.

"I really, really thought I should play the part of Emily," Holly continued. "But Diana said I wasn't plain enough."

Holly waved across the crowd at Diana, who was busy chatting to a bunch of stiff-necked Channel Eleven executives. Diana had petitioned strongly for Jessica, Holly and Blake and was thrilled they had won the roles. She looked back and smiled. A moment later Holly realised the insensitivity of her comment.

"Not that I'm saying you're plain!" she added, taking the time to look at Jessica. "I'm not saying that at all. And being plain isn't a bad thing anyway . . ."

"Don't worry," Jessica assured her. "I wanted to play Racine but they thought I looked too innocent."

Holly took this as a compliment. Jessica decided then and there that she liked her co-star. Holly reminded Jessica of herself a couple of years ago, even though they were both fifteen. Jessica matured faster than her peers and in many ways found it difficult to relate to them. Her ex-best friend Gabrielle often accused her of being a killjoy, though Jessica preferred to describe herself as reserved. Fortunately, Holly's energy was infectious. Jessica wished Gabrielle could see them now.

By this time, Holly's interest was on a woman making a grand entrance. Her dress was jaw-dropping, her voice deafening and her bleached blonde hair traffic-stopping.

"Oh my God! She looks so much older in real life!"

Holly was referring to Sadie Palmer, one of Australia's best known and loved soapie actresses. Holly pinched herself as she thought of all the letters she'd written to Sadie and the autographed photographs she'd received in return.

"I didn't know she was in this show," said Jessica.

"My agent reckons she's going to play my mum. Should I go over and say something? We will be working together every day."

Holly had made up her mind to introduce herself to Sadie when the band stopped playing and two muscle-clad lifesavers escorted Karen Wolfe to centre stage. She took the microphone confidently.

"Could I have everyone's attention please," she

began. The rowdy crowd came to a standstill. Holly was annoyed she'd missed a chance to meet Sadie.

"First of all, let me officially welcome you to the pre-production launch of *Bondi Place*. As you can see from the sights around you, we have the perfect location for a soap and I believe the perfect combination of people to make it a success."

The speech continued for the best part of an hour, with Karen raving about everything from theme music to on-set catering. While most of it was mumbo jumbo to Jessica and Holly, this was an exciting new world and it held their interest if nobody else's. Karen finally began to wind up when she noticed a network executive asleep on his deck chair.

"Last but not least I'd like to introduce our front-line. Without any further ado, let's say g'day to the stars of our show."

Jessica and Holly looked at each other nervously. Karen had told them they would be introduced around but neither expected it to happen on stage. One by one, in order of importance, Karen introduced the cast and asked them to join her. Geraldo was first, followed by Sadie and another soap veteran named Jared Hopper.

Ex-game show hostess turned actress Belinda Viola followed, then Rodney 'Rocket' Rogers, a well-known comedian who hatched a deal to play himself in the show. Each received varying applause, though Jessica was too numb and Holly too starstruck to clap. With eight cast members introduced, Karen paused and looked over to the girls.

"Now to three faces you won't have seen before," she said, her last words trailing into a worried stutter. "Well, I can see two of them. I'd like you to meet Jessica Fairgate who will be playing Emily and Holly Harrison who you'll soon know better as Racine."

All eyes were on Jessica and Holly as they made their way to the podium. While Holly revelled in the attention, Jessica felt like she was blindfolded. Up on the stage, the sun was like a spotlight in her eyes. Karen could see better but could still not find the figure she needed.

"Has anyone seen young Blake Dexter?" she asked, surveying the crowd. A network executive raised an eyebrow. It was most unprofessional of a young, inexperienced cast member to be absent from such an important event.

Standing higher on the podium, Karen looked down to the beach where a scruffy young man was arguing with a security guard. "There he is! There's our Stefan!" she said as the crowd followed her pointed finger all the way to Blake. Down below, Blake was desperately trying to talk his way in, having forgotten his invitation and run late because he couldn't find anything clean to wear. Karen waved to the security guard who allowed Blake to proceed. The crowd parted, but it wasn't only to get a good look at him. Blake's dirty and crinkled clothes were enough to set anybody back. By the time he reached the stage, Karen was having palpitations. Blake was supposed to play their resident hunk, but at the moment he looked more like a street kid who hadn't washed in weeks. For him there was no applause – just an unspoken consensus that this guy could be trouble. Feeling obliged to say something, Blake took the microphone.

"Sorry I'm late. Would you believe I was signing autographs?"

There was an uneasy silence, particularly from the suits in the executive corner. Karen quickly reached for her glass of champagne and encouraged everyone else to do the same. Meanwhile, Blake stepped back to where Holly and Jessica were standing. Though they didn't have the chance to speak, Blake could tell he hadn't made a good impression. Jessica, in particular, thought his behaviour was appalling and was angry at herself for finding him just remotely attractive.

Karen hurriedly raised her glass to propose a toast. "Here's to *Bondi Place*."

* * *

Jessica, Blake and Holly hardly saw each other for the remainder of the afternoon. Jessica spent most of her time talking to Michael Warner, the scheduled director of the first five episodes. She openly and honestly discussed her insecurities and Michael, recognising her obvious intelligence, did his best to appease her doubts. Holly spent the next couple of hours one step behind Sadie, meeting most of the crew instead. In sharp contrast, Blake copped a dressing-down from Karen, who instructed him to dress up in future and rethink his attitude. The only person who greeted him warmly was Diana, but even she reiterated

Karen's warning. Blake accepted he'd made a mistake and, with his charming-as-ever smile, promised to make a better effort in future. By the end of the day he was confident he had everyone wrapped around his little finger. Except, to his frustration, Jessica.

CHAPTER FOUR

NEW SOAP SET TO MAKE A SPLASH!

SYDNEY – Channel Eleven has announced the cast for its ambitious new soap *Bondi Place*.

The five-night-a-week drama will star Geraldo Mercardo, Sadie Palmer, Jared Hopper and former *Mystery Clue* hostess Belinda Viola. Rocket Rogers, whose comedy album *Funny Bone* is still among the top ten best sellers in the country, has also secured a role playing himself.

Bondi Place is tipped to premiere in an early evening time slot late next month. While producer Karen Wolfe remains tight-lipped about the concept of the show, industry watchers believe it will focus on the trials and tribulations of the residents of a Bondi Beach apartment block. Campbell Parade and the local surf club, where the cast and crew gathered for a party over the weekend, will also feature prominently.

"It's about life and love and good times," beamed Belinda Viola, who added some weight to the rumour that the soap may screen opposite *Mystery Clue*. "*Mystery* hasn't done so well since I left, so it would probably be a good time to attack!"

Belinda, who has been busy taking acting lessons since quitting the long-running game show, described her character as "the resident superbitch!" Geraldo, who announced his engagement to Norwegian air line stewardess Ulrika Walstrom at the party, is believed to be playing a rich and wealthy restaurant owner who sponsors the lifesaving club.

The show will also test the talents of three newcomers. Jessica Fairgate, Holly Henderson and Blake Dexter beat hundreds of hopefuls to win the lead teenage roles. Production will commence next week.

— *VANESSA SHARP*

"Holly Henderson!" Holly didn't care that the journalist had made a mistake with her surname. This was her first mention in the press and she knew many more would follow.

The taxi pulled into Channel Eleven, a multi-building complex in North Bondi just ten minutes from the beach. A massive transmission tower created a space station effect. Spiralling into the sky, it rocketed pictures to millions of homes. Holly considered her image breaking up into tiny pieces, then recomposing in television sets around the country. *Wow!*

She neatly folded the newspaper for her scrapbook and rifled through her bag for the taxi voucher which the production office had couriered to her the day before. Darren, her agent, had negotiated transport into her contract so she would be driven to and from the studio every day.

"Thanks Chan," she said as she signed the docket over and stepped out of the vehicle. "Say 'hi' to your wife and kids for me."

The taxi took off, leaving Holly standing on the front step. She took a brief moment to collect her thoughts, knowing the day ahead would be enormous and there would be much to learn and remember. *I can't believe I'm standing on the steps of Channel Eleven*! she marvelled to herself. Tracking her reflection as she approached the front door, she discreetly stood up straighter, shook her hair back, and strode confidently inside.

The foyer was a million dollar show in itself, opening to a spectacular glass ceiling which exposed three floors of office workers. Several television sets tuned to Channel Eleven punctuated the design, something like the set of a pop video. Portraits of network actors, newsreaders and even cartoon characters adorned the walls. There was even a shot of Zac Winter wearing a leather jacket and sitting on the set of his talk show *Teen Scene*. Holly hoped that her face would one day be up there, smiling next to his.

"Holly! Over here!" The voice belonged to Jessica, who was sitting in the waiting area. A young man named Scott was beside her. His job title was 'runner' and he was required to run errands and assist all departments. They'd all met at the barbecue. Holly thought Scott was cute. She loved his long, curly black hair.

"I'm the welcoming committee," said Scott. "When Blake shows up I'll take you down to Karen's office. She's got a big day planned for you."

"I'm so excited," said Holly. "How come you look so relaxed, Jessica?"

Jessica responded with a modest shrug. She was making a deliberate effort to suppress any whiff of excitement, fearing ego would follow. She knew this would be detrimental to the process of acting, so she was determined to stay calm and rational.

"Guess I'm just a good actress," she replied. "Did you receive your scripts?"

"You betcha! So much to memorise. And what about that scene where I call you a 'country cow' and tell you to go back to your paddock! I want to meet the person who wrote that one."

"You'll meet everyone," Scott assured her. "And a little tip from me. Be especially nice to the script department. It pays to have them on your side."

The girls made a mental note of the advice.

Holly couldn't help looking back at the life-size portrait of Zac on the wall. "Do you know him?" she asked Scott, pointing up to Zac.

Scott's face turned sour. "Yeah . . . unfortunately."

Before Holly could question this negative response, another voice entered the conversation.

"Excuse me, Scott," said one of four receptionists who sat behind the front desk of Channel Eleven. Each wore a headset and would have earache by the end of the day, having connected hundreds of calls and fielded complaints from irate viewers. Jessica remembered the time she'd phoned in to protest about the replacement of an Audrey Hepburn film with a football telecast and wondered if she'd blasted one of these girls. She was sorry if she had.

"Message from a Blake Dexter. He's running late."

*   *   *

"Running late?!" Karen recoiled.

They were standing in her office, which was actually a petitioned-off cubicle in a corner of the *Bondi Place* headquarters located at the west wing of Channel Eleven. Several other staff members worked furiously in the background. "I certainly hope he doesn't do this when we start shooting!"

Jessica felt embarrassed on Blake's behalf, which annoyed her. *Why should I feel bad because he can't get his act together*? she asked herself. The question she didn't want to analyse was why this guy, whom she'd met only once, was having such an explosive effect on her. For some reason he really made her blood boil.

Karen took a sip of water and calmed down. "At least I can count on the two of you. The reason I've asked you in today is to prepare you for next week. I'll take you around the studio and introduce you to some of the departments you'll be working with." She picked up a strand of Holly's long golden locks. "We might do something with this as well."

"Do you need me for anything else?" Scott asked.

"Just keep an eye out for Blake. When he arrives, direct him to the studio." Karen turned to the girls. "Buckle your seatbelts. You're about to undertake a crash course in the wonderful world of television."

* * *

Studio Four was a five minute walk from the administration and offices. The walls of the studio were constructed from grey aluminium sheeting and contained layers of insulation to stop the noise from outside intruding. Jessica and Holly were surprised that such a stark, factory-like environment was used for the production of glamorous television shows.

Karen stopped them at the door. A red light was flashing above it.

"This is where the interior scenes of *Bondi Place* will be filmed," Karen explained. "*Top Cops* is in production here until the end of the week. Then our show moves in."

Holly felt a shiver of excitement run up her spine. "I love *Top Cops*. It's a shame they're axing it."

"Don't mention it when you go inside," Karen explained. "Everyone is very upset."

The red light stopped flashing which meant the cameras had stopped rolling and it was safe to enter. Inside, Jessica and Holly tip-toed behind Karen, dodging masses of cables on the floor. A crew of fifteen were gathered around a brightly-lit set which Holly recognised as the police station from the show. It was much smaller than it appeared on screen and the actors – at one stage the most popular in the country –

were also much shorter than she imagined. Everyone was highly strung and emotional. Most of the crew were wearing headphones and paying as much attention to what they were hearing as to what they were doing. Karen pointed to a glass window up toward the roof.

"That's the control room," she whispered. "That's where the director sits. He calls all his instructions to his first assistant who passes the message on to the actors. That's him over there. His name is Gus. He'll be working on our show as well."

Karen pointed out a curly-haired man wearing baggy shorts and an old 'I've been to Ayers Rock' T-shirt. Sure enough, Gus seemed to be taking direction through his headset and responded by shouting, "Cut. We've got to go again."

Everybody sighed and moved back to their original positions. "What happened?" asked Holly. "I thought they said their lines really well."

"Probably a technical problem," Karen explained. "Get used to them. Shadows on the walls, faults in the sound. Sometimes you guys will do a fantastic performance but a technical hitch will ruin it."

Holly was about to ask another question when Gus shouted "Quiet" and listened to further instruction from up above. A few seconds later the message came through. "Okay Hayley, we want to see you enter."

Hayley, who played Detective McKee, opened the door to the wobbly set and waited outside. "Okay and action."

Before Hayley had the chance to move, the sound of a heavy door closing took everyone by surprise. It wasn't the door to the set.

"Hey – I've been looking for you guys everywhere!" hollered Blake as he spotted Karen, Holly and Jessica. He emerged from the shadows, completely unaware that he'd interrupted the filming of an important scene. Karen was so furious that she looked as though steam would pour out of her ears.

The assistant director removed his headphones. His angry superior could be heard shouting down the line. "Who the hell is that?! Get him out of here!"

Blake suddenly realised what he had done. *So that's what Scott meant about the flashing red light.*

* * *

"I'm really, really sorry," said Blake in a sincerely apologetic tone.

Karen was not convinced. "This isn't a playground, Blake. You're an actor employed to do a very important job. Thousands would kill to be in your position. Nobody on this show is indispensable."

The last line echoed in his head. Blake knew Karen was serious. He only wished he could express how serious he was about his job, even though his every action to date suggested the opposite. He could hardly tell Karen why he was late: that his father had promised to drive him to the studio but hadn't come home all night, that he'd spent all morning looking for him and finally located him asleep on a park bench after a wild pub crawl with his mates. No, he could hardly tell her that. The best he could do was to take the heat and make up for it in future.

The discussion was taking place in the video tape library, a room overloaded with footage from thirty years of Channel Eleven productions. Blake noticed a tape marked 'TV'S WORST ACTORS'. He recalled watching the show, a merciless yet high-rating compilation of the worst soapie actors over the years. Blake didn't want to end up in the next edition.

Karen opened the door into the busy corridor where Jessica and Holly were waiting. Blake believed that Jessica was somehow savouring the moment, as if she felt he deserved to get in trouble and was glad to witness it. This was half true: Jessica believed he had it coming but took no delight in observing it. She was far too concerned about the prospect of having to work with him on a daily basis.

Holly broke the tension. "Where to now?"

"Time to split you up," said Karen. "Follow me."

Holly kept pace with the producer but oncoming foot traffic forced Jessica and Blake to lag a little behind. Blake took advantage of the moment.

"You don't like me, do you?" he asked Jessica.

"Not particularly, no," was Jessica's cool reply.

* * *

Holly looked at her hair in the mirror. All she could think about was the Big Pineapple, a popular tourist attraction on the Queensland coast which she and her father had visited last Christmas. *My hair is the colour of the Big Pineapple!* she thought to herself.

"The camera will love it!" enthused Lulu, the hair and make-up artist who had just put the dye through Holly's hair. Lulu's own hair was testament to her skills as a colourist. All in all, a total of seven shades had infested her hair in the last three months and there wasn't a patch of her natural mousy brown regrowth in sight. She was currently pitch black right to the roots.

"Yeah, I'm slowly warming to it," Holly replied.

Little did Holly know it, but Lulu was fresh out of beauty college and somewhat over-enthusiastic. Karen had told her to "make Holly look more like Sadie Palmer's daughter" and Lulu had taken this direction to an extreme.

The conversation was interrupted by the arrival of the queen of pineapple hair herself – Sadie. She sat down in the chair next to Holly and caught her breath. She was fresh from a publicity photo shoot with Geraldo on the beach.

"That's it!" she declared. "I'm never going back to that beach again! I'll have it stipulated in my contract!"

Holly decided this was her golden opportunity to get to know Sadie. "What's the problem?" she asked.

"Sand! In my face, in my hair – I've even got it in my underwear!" she complained. "Every time I opened my mouth I got a meal of it!"

Holly couldn't help laughing. Sadie was over-the-top with a capital 'T', a true performer on-screen and off.

"Don't worry," said Holly. "Your hair still looks great."

Sadie reached to the back of her windswept head and began to tug. After a few pulls the entire mass of hair took flight. It was a wig! Underneath, Sadie's hair was cropped short and dark.

"Put this through the wash," said Sadie as she handed the wig to Lulu. "But don't tumble dry it. Hang it on the line instead!"

Holly nearly died on the spot. Sadie could see she was in shock.

"Close your mouth, sweetie," she said. "You'll be wearing carpet after a few months in that chair!"

Holly couldn't wait to write to her friends in Ballina and tell them that one. Meanwhile, Sadie reached into her handbag to retrieve her mobile phone, ejecting several bits and pieces in the process. Among the contents was a small photo frame decorated with gum tree nuts. A photo of Sadie and another man was squashed inside. Holly recognised it instantly.

"Where did you get that from?" she asked excitedly.

Sadie picked up the frame. "You mean this? Some fan sent it to me. Hideous, isn't it? That's me and my ex-husband. He had bad taste as well. I carry it everywhere to remember how much better off I am without him."

Holly felt like the biggest gum tree nut of all. The fan who had made the frame was none other than Holly. Worst of all, she'd filled it with a photo of herself which she could just see the edges of underneath.

"Can I have a closer look?" she asked. Sadie handed it over and continued to rifle through her bag. Holly needed only an instant to whip the frame under the table and remove the photo of herself. She handed it back, leaving Sadie none the wiser.

Holly screwed the photo into a ball and stashed it in her pocket. The gesture was symbolic. Out with the old, in with the new. The gum tree nut girl would never be seen again. The pineapple girl was here to stay.

* * *

Jessica sucked in her stomach and tried one last time to squeeze into the size eight dress. She finally managed to fasten the buttons at the front.

She stepped out from behind the curtain to show Leo the results. Leo was the wardrobe designer on *Bondi Place* and had spent all weekend searching through charity-shops for Emily's country bumpkin clobber. A little man with a big personality, he'd left Emily's wardrobe until last, preferring to allocate most of his budget to the designer threads of the more upmarket characters.

"I think it's a bit too tight," Jessica admitted. She didn't want to be any trouble but after her experience with Lulu, who cut her hair into an unflattering fringe, she thought it best to speak up. Though Leo could see it was busting at the seams, he knew the charity-shops would not exchange it for a bigger size and he had no budget left to buy new clothes.

"Skip lunch and you'll be fine," he suggested with a chuckle. "I'll also have a go with my needle and thread. Might be able to give you an extra inch or two."

Jessica still felt uncomfortable but didn't argue. She wouldn't have to wear the dress until her first scene on the beach next week and if she skipped every meal before then she'd probably get away with it. At least she didn't have to wear the skimpy bikini which was hanging on the rack marked 'Holly'. Then she'd have to starve for a month.

At that moment, Holly walked in, her hair illuminating the room. "Hi Jessica," she said, before extending her hand to Leo. "I'm Holly Harrison. I'm ready for my fitting."

Leo shook her hand. Holly should have been nervous but it was Leo who was trembling. Holly now looked very different to her audition tape and Leo was worried the colours he'd selected for Racine would no longer suit.

"I've just got to make a quick call," he said, making his way over to the phone.

"I feel like I'm riding the superloop," Holly quipped

to Jessica. "So many people to meet, so many names to remember. Love your hair. Your fringe looks excellent."

"Thanks," said Jessica, even though she thought quite the opposite. By this time Holly had discovered the bikini on the rack. She recognised it from the Elle MacPherson designer collection.

"Is that for me?" she asked. Jessica confirmed it with a sympathetic nod. But Holly held the skimpy garment against herself and looked in the mirror.

"I love it!" she declared. "I've never been able to afford anything from Elle's collection!"

"I'm glad it's you and not me," said Jessica as she reached over to feel a strand of Holly's hair. It was hard and brittle. Jessica dreaded to think of the chemicals that had gone into it.

In the background Leo was also worried. "Hi Karen. It's Leo," he said into the phone. "About this girl you've got doing hair and make-up. She's got to go!"

* * *

Claude DeSusa was the kind of man who made you feel out of breath before you had even opened your mouth. As publicist for *Bondi Place*, he had just warned Blake to expect endless hours of interviews, photo shoots and public appearances. Claude believed publicity was everything and that his was the most important job on the show. He was also an insatiable gossip.

"I've organised a photographer for your first scenes next week," he explained. "We'll get some shots of you riding the waves. I think it's a great angle, you being a professional surfer and all that. Have you won any titles?"

Blake was gobsmacked. *Pro surfer? Titles?* Clearly, Claude overestimated his ability. It was only then that he realised the publicist was referring to the question-naire he'd filled out at Carter Castings. At the time, Blake had thought it would be relatively harmless to list surfing as one of his skills. However, ticking the box marked 'professional' may not have been so smart. Truth was, he couldn't even stand up on a board.

"Um," Blake began weakly, searching for the right

words to break the unimpressive reality of it all.
"Thing is, I haven't actually *competed* as a professional."

"Long as you know what you're doing, that's the
main thing," Claude enthused. "Karen's thrilled that
she doesn't have to hire a stunt double."

No stunt double?! Blake had assumed a lookalike
would be hired to perform the surfing sequences but
this was evidently not the case. Claude's mobile phone
rang to interrupt the conversation. The caller was
Harvey, his photographer, reporting on the publicity
shoot with Sadie and Geraldo. Claude wasn't happy to
hear that Sadie had been difficult.

As Claude chatted, Blake desperately tried to think
of a way to dig himself out of the hole he was in.
Karen's warning echoed in his ears: *Nobody on this
show is indispensable*. He couldn't give her another
reason to dispense with him. He had one week before
the surfing scene and photo shoot. One week to
become an expert.

Claude concluded the call just as Karen popped her
head around the door.

"Everything okay?" she asked, looking directly at

Claude. It was as if she half-expected something to go wrong and was keeping a special eye on Blake.

"Terrific," Claude gushed. "This lad is going to be a star!"

"Let's hope so. I'm off to collect the girls to introduce them to their study tutor. You are free to go, Blake. I'll see you next week." And she was gone.

"Good producer," Claude commented. "But Karen is a Wolfe by name and a wolf by nature. Those fingernails turn into claws at the first hint of trouble."

Blake knew it. *One week. One week to become an expert.*

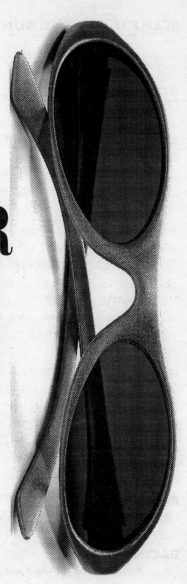

CHAPTER FIVE

SCENE 17.   EXT. BONDI BEACH   MORNING

STEFAN, RACINE, EMILY, N/S SURFERS

OPEN ON A WIDE SHOT OF THE OCEAN, MASSIVE WAVES ROLLING AND CRASHING INTO SHORE. THE CONDITIONS ARE SPECTACULAR, VOLATILE AND DANGEROUS. ONLY A FOOL OR A MADMAN WOULD ATTEMPT TO SURF IN THIS SWELL.

STEFAN RUNS DOWN TO THE WATER'S EDGE. AS THE COLD WATER INVIGORATES HIS BODY, HE JUMPS ON HIS BOARD AND PADDLES OUT TO THE BREAKERS. A SIX METRE WAVE BEGINS TO FORM AND HE RISES ON THE BOARD, SURFING THE TUBE AND STAYING WITH IT UNTIL IT BEGINS TO BREAK UP.

FROM THE SAFETY OF THE SAND, RACINE AND EMILY WATCH IN AWE. EMILY HAS NEVER SEEN ANYTHING LIKE IT. RACINE IS LESS IMPRESSED.

RACINE
Talk about a death wish.

EMILY
He's just . . . he's just so talented.

RACINE
He's a show off! You'll see plenty of them around Bondi Beach.

EMILY

They're not like the boys back home, that's for sure.

RACINE

Hurry on – you'd better get back to work. The lunch rush is just about to start.

BUT EMILY IS MESMERISED. BY THIS TIME, STEFAN IS RIDING ANOTHER MONSTER WAVE. RACINE GRABS HER BY THE ARM.

RACINE

Go on! You don't want me to have to fire you on your first day.

EMILY HEADS BACK OBEDIENTLY IN THE DIRECTION OF THE SURF CAFE. RACINE SETTLES ON THE SAND AND LOOKS OUT TO STEFAN.

RACINE

(TO HERSELF) Stupid girl. This is all your fault, Stefan Elliot. Don't think I'll let you get away with it.

FREEZE FRAME ON RACINE, A DEVILISH SMILE DAWNING ON HER FACE.

A cumulonimbus cloud hovered protectively in front of the sun, temporarily shrouding Bondi Beach in ominous grey. Jessica studied the sky through the window of the make-up van where Lulu was busy giving Holly a heavy coat of foundation. Jessica's make-up felt like plaster.

"I can't believe this day is finally here," she said, clutching her copy of the first episode script.

"Me neither," said Holly. "The last few weeks have been such a spin out. Seems like only yesterday we were auditioning at Carter Castings."

"Ta-da!" beamed Lulu, whose hair had suffered another chemical transformation since Jessica and Holly had last seen her. She was now a dark shade of grey. "You're ready to roll."

There was a rat-a-tat-tat on the door. Daniel, the first assistant location director, popped his head into the van. He was twenty-three and reminded Jessica of her older brother Adam. They both had uncontrollable curly black hair and fair, ivory-like complexions.

"Michael would like Emily and Racine on the beach," he said.

"This is it," said Holly as she reached out for Jessica's hand. "Our very first scene!"

* * *

The girls rehearsed their dialogue three more times as they walked from the make-up van parked on Campbell Parade down to the Channel Eleven crew at the south end of the beach. Even though it was only seven in the morning, the beach was alive with activity. Joggers and surfers had gathered to watch the filming.

"Are you nervous?" Jessica asked Holly.

"Nervous as I'll ever be. Are you?" Holly replied.

Jessica nodded and clutched her stomach. She was feeling a little queasy but didn't know if it was nerves or because she had skipped breakfast in order to squeeze into the sun dress.

Holly, too, felt uncomfortable wearing the bikini. "Do you reckon my boobs are too small?" she asked.

"Count yourself lucky," replied Jessica as, looking down, she considered her own lack of action in the breast department. "You're doing better than I am."

Michael Warner, the director, approached them

with a smile. "Slight change of plans. We're going to wait a few more minutes until we get a break in the clouds. Sunshine is essential for this scene."

Jessica and Holly were still grappling with the extent of Michael's job. As director, he made all the final decisions – from how they would perform their lines to how the cameraman would focus his lens. They had rehearsed for him an hour earlier and received very little in the way of criticism. Basically, he had asked them to slow down and suggested Holly ease her performance. She was making Racine too nasty. The girls then adjusted their delivery to his satisfaction. Holly felt more confident as a result; Jessica, however, refused to be lulled into a false sense of security. She knew it was an easy scene and much harder ones would follow.

"We'll probably shoot the sequence with Blake first," Michael continued. "Then it will be your turn to sweat!"

Michael moved away and began chatting to the cameraman. Further down the beach, Holly spotted Blake having his photo taken by Harvey. Claude was nearby.

"Look at him. He doesn't have any lines and didn't even have to rehearse. All he has to do is surf. He's got it easy," she complained.

Little did they know, Blake was more nervous than both of them put together. He'd spent the last seven days desperately trying to perfect the art of surfing and had made some progress. But, face-to-face with enormous waves, his confidence was eroding fast.

"How about you peel off the top of your wet suit," Claude suggested. "Karen wants beefcake shots. The teen magazines love this sort of stuff."

Blake obediently complied and began strutting a series of model poses, catching the attention of both Jessica and Holly. Suddenly, the sun came out, bathing the beach in golden orange. Michael rose quickly to his feet.

"Okay people, the sun is out. Time to play!" he said. "The swell is looking good. Let's get this surfing sequence over and done with."

This was good news for Holly and Jessica who were eager to start; bad news for Blake, who wished he could put the sequence off forever. Looking up at the sky, he saw the clouds were gone for good. There would be no further delay. He said a silent prayer while he was at it.

"We'll do more shots afterward if that's okay," said Claude to Michael. Publicists were often a pain in the neck during filming, but Claude was determined to stay on Michael's good side. "We won't get in the way, promise!"

"Right-o, Blake, you know the story," said Michael as he led Blake to a pre-determined mark on the sand. A six-foot high surf board was waiting for him. "Just as the script says. You carry the board down to the water, hop on and hopefully you'll be just in time to catch a monster wave. Should be easy for a pro surfer like you."

Before Blake could respond, another crew member zipped up his wetsuit. The cameraman loaded his equipment on his shoulder and prepared to track Blake down to the water. Thanks to the clouds, they were already running behind, so it was vital they complete this sequence as quickly as possible. All systems were go.

"And, action!"

Blake took a deep breath and made his way down to the breakers, the cameraman following closely behind.

One to one with the waves, his imagination unleashed, he perceived the ocean as a giant monster, opening its mouth to swallow him. The cold water tickled his toes and then struck him with a vengeance. He fell onto his board and began to paddle. So far so good. A gigantic wave appeared. Blake knew that this was the time to take to his feet but his body was frozen. The wave rolled right over him.

"Keep going," Michael shouted from the beach.

Blake continued to paddle. Another wave approached. This time he attempted to stand but was quickly toppled in a classic nosedive. The gathering watched as the wave sucked him under. The board hurled in the opposite direction. It was clear that Blake had no idea at all.

The onlooking surfers were laughing hysterically but all Jessica could think about was whether Blake would be okay. He surfaced without injury. Michael, meanwhile, was already weighing up the costs. He dialled a number on his mobile and waited.

"Karen? It's Michael. Afraid we have a bit of a problem. I hope we can afford a stunt double for Stefan because we need one down here right away!"

Blake made his way slowly back to the shore. The crew had once again settled onto the sand. He turned to Jessica and Holly, hopeful of some sympathy. But Holly was already making use of the delay by striking a pose for Harvey. Jessica had long since overcome her concern and regarded him with icy disdain. Blake assumed correctly that she thought he was the biggest loser on the planet.

"In the meantime we'll do the girls," Michael said. Blake approached him full of remorse.

"Must be having a bad day," he said sheepishly.

"How many titles did you say you'd won?" Michael wondered out loud.

It was a rhetorical question. Fortunately, Michael had a sense of humour.

* * *

Rush hour at the Channel Eleven cafeteria: all but a few tables were occupied, with actors, newsreaders and the occasional pop star enjoying lunch. The conversation loud and echoing. The cafeteria had once been a sound stage and there was not a single window. Fake plants failed to improve the ambience.

Holly and Sadie waited patiently in line at the counter. Having come straight from Studio Four, they were wearing dressing gowns. Holly felt dowdy and faintly embarrassed that so many famous faces would have their first glimpse of her looking like this.

"Are you sure I did okay?" Holly asked Sadie. Despite the potential for star spotting, her main priority was on the performance she had just given.

Sadie touched her hand reassuringly. "Listen, honey, you did better than my first time in a studio. I had to bawl my eyes out but I was so cold and nervous that my tears were frozen!"

"I guess so. But the scene shouldn't have been difficult. All I had to do was laugh at the right time but I couldn't even do that. I thought Michael was going to murder me!"

"I've worked with Michael before. He's usually a pussycat. He's just uptight because we're doing the first episode. Everyone's a bit stressed."

Holly appreciated the advice. But her attention was captured by the arrival of the one and only Zac Winter. He was wearing exactly the same clothes she had seen in his portrait in the network foyer – black jeans, white T-shirt and leather jacket.

"Oh my God!" said Holly to Sadie. "There he is! I can't believe it! I'm going to die!"

Zac grabbed a tray and sauntered past, a distinctive cologne wafting through the air. Holly thought she had died and gone to heaven.

Sadie tapped him on the shoulder as he passed by. "Hey, you! Ever heard of lining up?"

Zac played dumb. "Sorry. I didn't realise this was a queue."

He looked at Holly and smiled, before backtracking to the end of the line.

"Did you see that?" Holly whispered to Sadie. "He smiled at me!"

Sadie rolled her eyes. "That is one incredibly rude young man."

Holly grabbed hold of the rail to stop herself from fainting. "He can be rude to me any time."

* * *

Studio Four had undergone quite a transformation. The *Top Cops* sets had been replaced by the bright interiors of *Bondi Place* – the insides of the apartments, cafe and Surf Club which would house the characters of the show. The first thing Jessica noticed was that the inside of the Surf Club didn't match the reality outside. Doors and windows were in different places. She hoped the viewers wouldn't notice.

Even though it was the third day of filming, this was Jessica and Blake's first time working in the studio. Their scenes to date had been at various locations around Bondi and with other actors. Apart from a brief moment in the make-up room, this was their first proper encounter since shooting the very first scene on the beach.

"How are you doing, Jessica?" Blake asked as they collided on their way to the Surf Cafe set.

"Fine, thanks," Jessica replied. "Do you need a stunt double for when you toss the apron?"

Jessica was referring to the moment at the end of the scene, which they had both performed in the audition. Blake felt Jessica's tone was patronising, even though she was joking.

"Only if you can't catch it," he replied. "Some people can give but they can't take."

Jessica felt the razor-sharp undercurrent. Thankfully, at that moment Holly bubbled onto the set. Now a veteran of five scenes in the studio – all with Sadie – she carried herself like a seasoned professional.

"How are my two favourite co-stars?" she asked.

Jessica rolled her eyes. Blake offered a sarcastic smile. By this time they were all standing in the middle of the brightly-lit set.

"Never mind. Let's talk about me. Guess who I met yesterday?" Holly continued.

Jessica and Blake looked blank.

"Zac Winter, of course!" Holly beamed.

"Keep the noise down," said Joe, one of the three camera operators. His round, bearded face could hardly be seen behind the imposing cameras which were mounted on platforms, enabling them to rotate up, down and around.

"I'll tell you the rest later," Holly whispered.

Gemma, the perky on-set hair and make-up girl, approached Holly with a comb. "You've got some sand in your hair, sweetheart," she said, taking Holly aside.

"Slight delay," Joe went on. "Five minute break everyone."

Jessica and Blake waited on set, sitting at separate tables. It was obvious to everyone that they weren't getting along. Blake was aware that they had started on the wrong foot and wanted desperately to rectify the situation. *But what do I say?* he asked himself. *When in doubt, compliment.*

"That dress really suits you," he said.

Far from being flattered, Jessica took offence. She hated the dress and Blake's intentions were fairly transparent. "No it doesn't," she responded.

Blake was taken aback. Every other person he knew loved to receive compliments. "You shouldn't be so hard on yourself."

"Maybe you shouldn't be so soft on yourself."

It was a direct hit and Blake knew it. He couldn't understand why Jessica was being so cold. Similarly, Jessica was at a loss to understand her hostility. It was as if she had no control over the words coming out of her mouth. She could only see it as a classic personality clash.

Fifteen minutes later Gus shouted "Action" and the scene was rehearsed and played to near perfection. Only three takes were necessary – quite impressive since it was the first time all three actors had performed together in the studio. The first take was insufficient because Holly rushed her lines. The second was almost spot on, except Blake fluffed a line and there was a slight audio hitch.

Karen watched the third and final take on the television monitor in her office, which was continuously tuned to the cameras in the studio. She was pleasantly surprised that the kids did so well, but another observation left her with a worrying knot in her stomach. It was something only the most experienced of producers would be able to detect – a potential disaster in the making.

* * *

Jessica and Blake waited on the couch in Karen's office, both nervous about the reason they'd been summoned.

"Sorry to keep you waiting," said Karen as she returned to her desk. "We're having a few problems on location. Geraldo crashed a dune buggy."

Blake was pleased to hear it. It reassured him to

know he wasn't the only person who'd stuffed up.

"First of all, I don't want either of you to panic. You're not here because you're in any kind of strife," Karen continued.

Jessica and Blake breathed a sigh of relief.

"Well, not this time," she added, looking directly at Blake. "I thought it would be helpful for you to know a little of what we've got in store for your characters. We don't normally tell the actors what's coming up too far in advance but in your cases I think we should make an exception."

Jessica's mind jumped to the worst possible conclusion. *Are we to be killed off in a car accident? Drowned in a tidal wave*? In the few seconds that it took Karen to go on, Jessica considered every possible horror scenario except the one in store.

"You see, the writers have decided that Emily and Stefan would make the perfect couple. You'll be working very closely together in coming weeks . . . or, should I say, very intimately."

Intimately?! Jessica could feel her stomach churning as if she might throw up at any second. Blake wasn't pleased about the prospect either. Karen could see the

potential for fireworks. She'd seen it seething in sub-
text on the monitor; now it was simmering before her
very eyes.

"These kinds of story-lines are always hard for
actors, especially those who don't know each other
very well. Needless to say, it's important that you
form a positive working relationship in order to
make it credible on screen. I'm not suggesting you
fall in love for real, just use the next couple of weeks
to support and get to know each other better," she
said.

Jessica was speechless. Blake decided this was his
opportunity to ingratiate himself with Karen once and
for all. "We'll do our best," he assured her. "I'm sure
Jess and I will become great mates."

Jessica was like a time bomb waiting to explode. For
some reason Blake found this very attractive. Jessica
was a challenge and he took the opportunity to push
her even further.

"Isn't that right Jess?" he said.

Jessica knew he had her over a barrel and it took all
her acting skills to agree. "Sure. Great mates."

The conversation was interrupted by Scott. "Excuse

me, Karen," he said. "The insurance company rep is here. It's about the dune buggy."

"You'd better bring him through." She returned her attention to Blake and Jessica. "I'm glad we had this little talk. Claude will need to see you at some stage as well. We're planning lots of publicity on this."

Publicity? Jessica dreaded the thought. Karen's phone rang and she picked it up, waving them out of her office. Outside, Blake attempted to ease the tension.

"Kind of funny, isn't it?" he said. Clearly, Jessica didn't think it was a laughing matter. "C'mon, Jess. Don't you think we ought to try and get along?"

Jessica paused to make sure her words struck him loud and clear. "Remember, we're only acting. And would you please stop calling me Jess!"

* * *

The Green Room of a television show is the common area for cast members, where they can relax and memorise lines in between scenes. Holly expected the *Bondi Place* variety to be equipped with modern appliances and a limitless supply of biscuits and cake. Instead, she found a disused office furnished with a couple of chairs from old talk show sets. Nonetheless, it was an excellent place to chat to fellow cast members and for this reason Holly hadn't even attempted her maths homework. She didn't care that her tutor was expecting it to be finished in a few minutes time.

"I used to watch *Mystery Clue* every night," she beamed at co-star Belinda Viola, a leggy blonde with false blue contact lenses. "Until you left, of course."

"I wish people would stop mentioning that show!" Belinda complained. Holly was somewhat taken aback. Evidently Belinda didn't like to be reminded of her game show past.

"I'm sorry," said Holly. "I didn't mean to offend you."

Belinda realised she had overreacted. She produced a letter she'd stuffed into the back of the chair. "I guess I'm having a bad day. I just got this from some loony tune who wrote that I can't cut it as an actress. A lot of people around here feel the same way."

Holly could see a tear forming in the corner of her

eye. She touched Belinda's hand reassuringly. "Don't listen to them. I saw that scene you did with Jared this morning. You were great."

Belinda smiled her thanks. Holly was surprised that such a famous and outwardly confident person could be so insecure on the inside. At that moment Jessica burst through the door.

"Holly! I've got to talk to you!" she said in a flustered tone of voice.

Belinda looked at her watch. "Yikes. I'm supposed to be doing a phone interview. Gotta fly." She touched Holly's shoulder on her way out. "Thanks for the therapy."

Jessica sat down and tried to calm down.

"What's the big crisis?" asked Holly.

"The writers are turning Stefan and Emily into a couple. That means Blake and I will have to do love scenes together!"

Holly couldn't resist a chuckle. "How cute. Just like Romeo and Juliet."

"More like Marge and Homer Simpson," said Jessica. "I can't do it. I don't know why but I can't stand the sight of him."

"I know why," Holly said with a smile. "Deep down you really like him."

Jessica scoffed. "How could you possibly think a thing like that?"

"URST," replied Holly. "Sadie told me all about it. It stands for Unresolved Sexual Tension. She reckons that's the case between her and Geraldo. Opposites attract, that kind of thing."

Jessica was in shock. *URST?! Between Blake and me?!*

"I've watched the two of you," Holly continued. "You hardly know each other, yet you're determined to fight. Am I right?"

Jessica thought it over. "He just rubs me up the wrong way, that's all."

Holly checked her watch and realised she was late for her tutoring session. "I'd love to stay and chat but I've got to run. Think it over."

Holly dashed out of the room. Jessica thought about Holly's analysis for a few seconds before emphatically dismissing the possibility. *No way, no chance, not ever*, she told herself. She took out her folder and proceeded to do her homework.

* * *

Algebra. Holly hated it. Here she was, at the age of fifteen, starring in what may well become the biggest hit on television and she was forced to worry about algebra. She couldn't keep her mind on it at all.

"I give up," she declared. "Is it lunch time yet?"

"Now you listen to me," said Hettie MacDonald, tutor to all the juvenile actors at Channel Eleven. "I've taught more kids with stars in their eyes than you've had hot dinners. I've seen them come and go but the only ones who have really made it are those who have kept up with their studies. You may think this business is all glamour and parties but it's not. It's a never-ending exam. If you don't keep your head on your shoulders you're likely to lose it. And the only place you'll find it again is in the unemployment office."

Hettie knew what she was talking about. A no-nonsense woman in her late fifties, she'd worked at Channel Eleven for over twenty years, tutoring one young star after another. She was renowned for being a strict disciplinarian, a competent examiner and, although Holly would find it impossible to believe, the life and soul of every network Christmas party. Holly had secretly nicknamed her 'Myrtle' after the pet piglet she had had as a child. In some ways Hettie looked like Myrtle – round face, sticking out ears and a pinkish complexion.

"I expect you to answer these questions by tomorrow morning."

"But I've got to learn my lines . . ."

"Tomorrow morning!"

Holly realised there was no point arguing. Hettie had more bite than any of her teachers at Ballina High and she was genuinely afraid to answer back. She sheepishly gathered her text books and left the classroom, which was actually a caravan parked at the back of the studio. She bumped into Jessica on her way out.

"Watch out," Holly warned in a low voice, although Hettie's antennae were tuned to every word. "She's been popping her commando pills again."

Holly headed back toward the studio, leaving Jessica to settle in for her session. Hettie was pleased to see her.

"Thank goodness. A dedicated student!" Hettie sighed.

This was Jessica's second session and she'd made quite an impression on the teacher. She handed over a page of answered questions.

"Well done," said Hettie as she read over the homework. "Looks like you got most of them right."

Jessica was disappointed. She was used to getting them all right. Clearly, her workload was making it impossible to concentrate on study even on a part-time basis. Add the pressure of having to do a romantic story-line with Blake and the situation was sure to get worse.

CHAPTER SIX

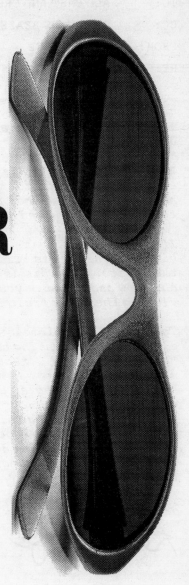

MEMORANDUM

TO: ALL CAST AND CREW

CC: SIR ANGUS BEAZEL

FROM: KAREN WOLFE

RE: FIRST EPISODE SCREENING

It's hard to believe we are now in our third week of filming!

As you are all aware, the editing process is long and hard but our skilful cutters have promised to have a rough version of the first episode ready for viewing by the end of the week!

I'm thrilled to invite you all to a special pre-view screening this Friday evening at six pm in the auditorium. This is an historic moment for our show and I'm sure you share my excitement in viewing the first fruit of our hard labour.

To mark this significant occasion, I have great pleasure in announcing the presence of Sir Angus Beazel, Managing Director of Channel Eleven. Although Sir Angus has not visited the set, he has played an integral part in the development of the show and is looking forward to meeting you all. Sir Angus has also promised to make the announcement we've all been speculating about -- the exact timeslot and debut date for the show. For all the punters among you, start placing your bets!

Looking forward to seeing you Friday evening.

Karen Wolfe

Blake read the memo sitting in the sand of Bondi
Beach on a fluorescent green bean bag. He imagined
Sir Angus as a short, overweight, balding man sucking
on a fat cigar. The picture brought a smile to his face.

"That's what we like," said Harvey as he clicked the
shutter on his multi-lens camera. "A kid without a
worry in the world."

Snapping back to the task at hand, Blake felt he had
plenty to worry about. He'd survived a lot of silly
modelling assignments but this scenario took the cake.
*Whose stupid idea was it to do a photo shoot with bean
bags on the beach anyway?* he thought to himself.

Claude, the proud organiser of the event, appeared
holding a bright yellow umbrella. Jessica and Holly
followed wearing matching polkadot swimsuits. Lulu
had just styled their hair and make-up. Jessica felt like
a reject from an ancient American beach bunny movie,
the kind they show on low-rating Saturday afternoons.
She took minor consolation from the fact that Blake
was wearing an equally crazy Hawaiian shirt. Holly,
however, thought it was all a big hoot.

"I reckon my boobs have grown," said Holly to
Jessica. "What do you think?"

"I don't know how," Jessica replied. "I've lost four kilos in the last three weeks. And I'm not getting any sleep. Did you see that two minute speech I have to perform with Geraldo tomorrow?"

Claude overheard Jessica's last comment. "I know, I know," he said. "You've got lines to learn. Publicity is just as important, you know. Unless the public see these pretty shots in the magazines they won't even watch *Bondi Place*!"

Jessica was not convinced. Her performance was her first priority. But, wary of inciting trouble, she held her tongue. She decided then and there that she would stay up late that night to learn the dialogue.

"Don't the girls look great?" Claude beamed.

A young photographer with greater ambitions, Harvey regarded taking publicity shots for *Bondi Place* as a means to an end. He'd decided it was profitable to agree with Claude no matter what. "Yeah. Cute as pumpkin pie."

"Let's get started," said Claude. "I'm after some fun, happy-go-lucky shots. Life's a beach and then you die, that kind of thing!"

Claude was in his element. While Jessica had serious

doubts and felt uncomfortable in the skimpy one-piece, Holly couldn't wait to get in front of the camera. This was their first staged publicity shoot and she was determined to look her best. Blake was playing it all very cool.

Lulu joined them with a large bag containing a seemingly endless array of props – everything from lollipops to frisbees. Jessica noticed the bubbly rapport between Claude and Lulu. It confirmed all her suspicions – they were both aliens from Planet Zany.

The shoot progressed with increasing lunacy, attracting a crowd of amused beach-goers before the first roll of film was in the can. Holly proved a natural, playing up to the camera and upstaging Jessica most of the time. Jessica didn't mind at all, which was of some concern to Claude. Eventually he pulled her aside.

"You're supposed to look happy," he said. "You love Bondi Beach, you love life. That's what we're trying to sell with this show."

Jessica knew he was right. Although she felt the concept for the shoot was sexist and demeaning, she understood it was her job to sell the image. She realised too that her fair skin was beginning to burn.

"Can I have a break to put on some more sunscreen?" she asked. Claude's mind ticked over and he smiled.

"Better idea," he said, turning back to Harvey, who was busy taking shots of Blake and Holly tossing the frisbee. "We've got enough of that. Let's get Blake rubbing sunscreen into Jessica's back."

Jessica wished she hadn't opened her big mouth. Blake and Holly came over. "What do you want me to do?" said Holly. "Maybe I could pretend to drown in the background?"

"I think you can stay out of this one," said Claude. Holly overcame the rejection in an instant and used her break to allow Lulu to touch up her make-up.

Claude lay a towel on the sand and instructed Jessica and Blake to sit. Blake noticed Jessica was covered in goose bumps. She felt uneasy with his close physical proximity.

"We're gonna have to get used to this," he reminded her. "I'm not that bad you know."

Blake had a point. The latest batch of scripts required Emily and Stefan to do several scenes together, something they hadn't had to do very much during the first three weeks. *Grin and bear it*, Jessica told herself.

"Okay, Blake, shirt off," said Claude.

Jessica watched as Blake unbuttoned his shirt. She couldn't help thinking about Holly's theory. *Do I really have the hots for him?* she asked herself. Looking at his tanned and muscular body, she had to admit he was attractive.

Blake caught a glimpse of her admiring eye. "Don't get too excited," he wisecracked.

Jessica found his joke highly egotistical. Any physical attraction she felt for him was instantly cancelled out by his personality. "No problem," she replied pointedly.

As Harvey clicked away, Blake applied lotion to Jessica's shoulders. It was cold and it tickled. She tried to fight it but couldn't help but laugh.

"That's it!" beamed Claude. Blake could sense Jessica relaxing. *The ice maiden thaws!* he thought. But only a little – and not on purpose, he reminded himself.

* * *

The atmosphere was tense in Studio Four. Geraldo was forty-five minutes late and Michael was absolutely furious. It was the last scene of a fifteen hour day and everyone was exhausted.

"Damn that man!" he said vehemently as he paced the Surf Club set. "He has no respect for any of us. Reckons he can come and go whenever he wants."

The crew agreed with his sentiments. Jessica, who had played several scenes opposite Geraldo so far, was also beginning to tire of his lazy attitude. She was especially anxious on this occasion as she had stayed up most of the night learning the two minutes of angry dialogue which Emily was scripted to speak to Geraldo's character, Stavros.

Five minutes later, Geraldo sauntered on to the set. "Sorry I'm late," he said in a voice which suggested he couldn't have cared less. "Traffic was terrible."

The crew watched intently as Michael approached him. They were all hoping for fireworks. Michael was in the mood to deliver but summoned all of his strength to resist.

"We have five minutes to do this scene," he said, through gritted teeth. "I hope you know your lines."

Geraldo took his mark on the set next to Jessica. "I'm going to teach you how to improvise," he whispered quietly.

Jessica realised Geraldo didn't know his lines after all. Before she had time to think, Michael yelled: "Stand-by and action."

Geraldo launched into a rough variation of the scripted dialogue. His delivery was confident and natural – he understood the point of the scene and was getting the message across. Jessica, however, was lost. With Geraldo making up his own lines she had no idea when to speak. Michael appreciated her problem, but faced with a choice of trying to instruct either Jessica or Geraldo, he knew it was much less trouble to concentrate on Jessica. He pulled her aside.

"Sorry to do this, kid," he began. "We're going to have to cut your big speech."

Michael grabbed a marking pen from his pocket and crossed out four of Emily's six paragraphs of dialogue. He then pointed to the two remaining sections. "You say this and let Geraldo do the rest of the talking," he said.

Jessica was devastated. "I spent hours learning this scene," she said.

"I know," Michael replied. "And I appreciate it. But you-know-who has no idea, so if we try and stick to the script we'll be here for hours."

Jessica realised protest was useless. She thought about Claude's emphasis on publicity the day before. At the time she couldn't wait to get home and learn her lines, believing that it was more important. Now, thanks to Geraldo's slackness, all her hard work was wasted. *It's not about how hard you work*, she warned herself. *It's how you play the game.*

* * *

No expense had been spared in transforming the Channel Eleven auditorium into an indoor water-world: seats had been set aside for a volleyball court, imitation palm trees planted in every corner and a bright yellow umbrella placed atop a giant television set for all to see. Even hired waiting staff were wearing *Bondi Place* T-shirts. The atmosphere was one of nervous anticipation. The first episode would provide the first real indication of whether the show would be a hit or a total turkey.

"Where on earth is he?" Karen moaned. The screening was scheduled to begin in fifteen minutes and Sir Angus still hadn't appeared. If he didn't turn up it would be akin to saying Channel Eleven didn't really care about the show.

"Can't wait to see our scenes," Blake said as he moved over to sit next to Jessica. "I hope nobody notices my stunt double!"

Jessica was surprised to hear Blake taking the mickey out of himself. In fact, she was surprised that they'd been getting along well all week. They had performed several scenes together and not argued once. Blake had known all his lines and delivered them with professionalism. Despite this turnaround, she was wary. He was a little too confident. She half suspected that he was trying to win her over and would revert to type the moment she succumbed.

"Wonder where Holly is?" she said.

Her question was soon answered. Holly appeared to join them, saying cheerfully, "Hi guys."

Outside, the Channel Eleven helicopter landed on the launch pad. The chopper was usually full of news reporters but this time its cargo was even more important. Karen was relieved to see Sir Angus Beazel step onto the tarmac, his hand firmly on his head to stop his toupee from taking flight in the ensuing cyclonic wind. He looked much older and frailer than his portrait in the foyer.

It took him a few minutes to make his way inside. There was no need for Karen to use the microphone. Silence was immediate and everyone was on their best behaviour. Karen introduced Sir Angus and ushered him to centre court.

"I'm very pleased to be here," he began, still trying to find his bearings. "I believe this show . . . this show . . . um . . ." he struggled to remember its name. "Er . . . *Bondi Place* will be a great, great success."

Karen was the first to applaud. Without further ado, she handed Sir Angus the remote control to start the video recorder, asking him to do the honours. He hit the fast forward button and the crowd erupted in uncontrollable laughter as the first scene began at a frenetic pace. Karen took control, rewinding the tape to start again at proper speed. At the same time, she assured Sir Angus that it was an easy mistake to make.

Everybody watched intently as the first scene featuring Sadie and Geraldo appeared on screen. Their performances were convincing, if distinctly similar to every other role they had played in the past. A scene between Belinda, Rocket and Jared was next. Belinda's performance was under intense scrutiny but she passed with flying colours, and seemed well on her way to abandoning the 'game show hostess' curse. Jessica, Holly and Blake waited anxiously for their first scene, the fourth in the episode. It was the 'Emily applies for the job' scene in the Surf Cafe. Holly could see the bright lights of Hollywood as she watched herself for the first time on television. Blake wasn't fussed one way or the other. He made a point of not judging himself. Jessica, however, studied her every breath and movement. She wished she'd done almost everything differently – from the way she walked into the room to the way she smiled at the end.

The episode was over twenty-three minutes later. The commercials would fill the remainder of the half hour on screen. The general consensus was positive. The show had a youthful, upbeat mood and the beach looked spectacular. Clearly, Sir Angus was not going to stay much longer, so Karen suggested he make his announcement about the premiere date and timeslot straight away. Rocket had been taking bets all week from cast and crew and the odds favoured a seven pm timeslot, beginning four weeks away. Everyone waited anxiously as Sir Angus referred to his notes.

"After a meeting with the Board of Directors in Melbourne earlier this week, I'm pleased to announce that *Bondi Place* will screen in the six-thirty pm time-slot from Monday to Friday, starting in two weeks time."

The room became deathly silent. *Six-thirty*?! Karen could hardly believe her ears. *Opposite the Channel Thirteen news*? *It was suicide*! Across the room, Claude fell dramatically back in his chair. *Two weeks from now! Only two weeks to kick the publicity machine into overdrive*?

Jessica, Blake and Holly could only draw on the reactions of the others to form their conclusions. They could see that the six-thirty timeslot was a problem spot for the network. Several shows had folded in this position over recent years. Rocket was the only person unfazed.

"I wonder if Channel Thirteen will put us on the

news when we get axed!" he joked in typically bad taste. Unlike the others, Rocket had a lucrative career as a stand-up comedian and didn't really care about the show. Examining the betting roster, he identified only one winner. He approached Blake with an envelope full of cash.

"You've won, babycake!" he said. "You're the only person who guessed both the timeslot and the date!"

Blake accepted the cash happily. It had been a wild guess and he hadn't anticipated winning. Rocket couldn't resist offering a tip.

"I'd stash it in my bottom draw if I were you. Unemployment could be just around the corner!"

Jessica, Holly and Blake shared an uneasy exchange. All of a sudden the future wasn't looking so bright.

CHAPTER SEVEN

AN INVITATION

CHANNEL 11 ELEVEN DRAMA PRODUCTIONS

have great pleasure in inviting

Ms Vanessa Sharp
Remote Control

to the media launch of their exciting
new drama serial

BONDI PLACE

on board the ferry
'Bondi Pride'

A banquet lunch and entertainment
will be provided.
Departure from Circular Quay 11 am.
Please contact Claude DeSusa
at Channel Eleven for further details.

Melbourne has always been the capital of 'four seasons in a day', but on the day of the all-important media launch of *Bondi Place*, Sydney was vying with its southern rival for the title. Jessica stood on the upper deck of the majestic passenger ferry 'Bondi Pride' and looked over to the Opera House. A bolt of lightning flashed in the thick dark cloud behind it. The sight was truly awesome.

"Kind of sums it up," said a voice very like Blake's. Turning around, she saw it was indeed Blake. He looked great, in trademark blue jeans and white T-shirt. Jessica was also dressed in blue and white. They were the only figures on deck.

"What do you mean?"

"This weather. Sunny at dawn, stormy by mid-morning. Just like us."

Jessica was amazed that something so observant and poetic could come from Blake. But she had to agree that his description of their relationship was apt. Summer and winter. Hot and cold.

"I guess so," she replied. "Have the journos started to arrive?"

"You bet. Claude sent me to find you. He's working

up to a nervous breakdown. I think it's because of the rain."

Jessica was amused. In Claude's view, today was the most important day in the life of the show. Journalists from all the major magazines and newspapers would be on board to interview the cast, having watched hastily-edited preview tapes of the first episode. Claude had allocated a cabin or deck to each publication and organised a rotating schedule for the actors during the three-hour cruise. He had issued several memos to emphasise how vital it was that all actors made a good impression. And, in Blake's case, he'd even issued seven pages of answers to likely questions for him to memorise. Blake took offence at the implication that he couldn't speak for himself, and used the document, suitably rolled, to swat the flies that bothered him as he watched television the night before.

"I guess it's too late to jump overboard," Jessica joked.

"You don't like the fame game, do you?" Blake observed. Jessica intrigued him. Most actors he'd come to know – most notably Sadie – revelled in attention, but Jessica seemed to shy away from it all.

"I'm not in this for all that," she said bluntly.

Blake didn't get the chance to find out more. Claude was hot on their trail.

"Here you are! The VIPs are arriving. Your pretty faces are supposed to be downstairs. That means now!"

* * *

Vanessa Sharp was a legend at this lunch. Claude allocated the *Remote Control* magazine columnist a prime position on the ferry, within easy-reaching distance of the sumptuous banquet and directly opposite the acoustic guitar set. Vanessa had attended thousands of media launches and was difficult to impress, but the prawn she was munching on was delicious and was steering her toward a favourable review.

"So is that your natural hair colour?" she asked Holly, who was doing her best to be poised and gracious. The question threw her entirely. Claude hadn't covered this one in his briefing.

"Er . . . um . . . not exactly," she replied into Vanessa's dictaphone. "They wanted my hair to be the same colour as Sadie Palmer's wig."

Vanessa nearly choked on her prawn. "Sadie Palmer wears a wig?!"

Holly realised she'd just divulged one of the best kept secrets in showbusiness. "Whoops . . . did I say that?"

Vanessa made a note. She only ever did so if it were important, just in case the dictaphone malfunctioned. Across the deck, Claude was watching with interest. Holly smiled to assure him everything was going wonderfully.

"So, how do you get along with Sadie?" Vanessa continued as she glanced at Sadie, being interviewed by a rival journalist nearby.

Holly decided this was an opportunity to make up for her slip-up. "She's the best. I love her. She's very down-to-earth. And there's nothing false about her at all!"

Vanessa laughed at Holly's unintentional pun. "Nothing except her hair," she said with a giggle.

Holly smiled awkwardly. Vanessa suspected that the

inexperienced newcomer would be a very useful source
of information in the future.

* * *

The ferry chugged lazily toward the heads, the land
which enclosed and protected the serene Sydney Harbour from the Pacific Ocean. The most expensive and
beautiful homes in Sydney were on display in all
directions on the harbour's edge.

The sun had re-emerged and many of the journalists
had relocated to the top deck, much to Claude's
distress. Convinced the clouds would linger, he'd set
the food and entertainment downstairs. Another buffet was being quickly established upstairs, under his
terse direction.

Blake was charming the shoulder pads off Nesley
Davies, the man-eating editor of *TV Hunks* magazine.
Nesley was the life of every launch and a shameless
flirt. She loved her job and accepted happily that she
would never write for a more credible publication.

"So, how do you feel about being TV's next pin-up
boy?" she asked, taking another sip of champagne.

Blake flashed a devilish smile. "I'm not sure. Do the staples hurt when you put them in?"

Nesley erupted in ferocious laughter. "Not when I do the job personally!"

Blake clicked his fingers, directing a passing waiter to top up Nesley's glass.

The editor was impressed. "So tell me, do you have a girlfriend?"

"Not at the moment."

"I'm sure you get plenty of offers. What do you look for in a girl?"

Blake's response was cheeky and calculated at winning her heart once and for all. "I'm not looking for a girl. I'm looking for a woman."

* * *

Jessica had been talking for so long that she'd forgotten the question. Three minutes ago she was rambling about the balance of trade, now she was offering her prediction for the date of the next federal election. It was only when she spotted a waitress carrying a platter of mini meat pies with decorative

Australian flags that she remembered what she was talking about.

"And that's why I don't think Australia should become a republic," she concluded.

Jim Mapleton, a journalist with a small community newspaper, was impressed with her views. Claude, who overheard the topic of conversation, was not.

"I'm afraid it's time to move on," he said, grabbing Jessica firmly by the hand. "Vanessa from *Remote Control* is ready to talk to you. About the show – not the republican debate."

"Thank you Jessica," Jim said. "I hope to talk to you again."

Fat chance of that, Claude thought to himself as he hustled Jessica away. Jim was relatively insignificant in the publicity scheme of things and had only scored an invitation to make up the numbers because Geraldo had refused to attend. Geraldo had had a raging argument with Karen over the issue, arguing it wasn't within his contractual obligations. In fact, he was afraid the press would ask questions about current investigations into his finances by the tax department. The possibility was so undesirable that Karen finally agreed to exclude him from the floating media circus.

"Sorry about him," said Claude to Jessica as he looked around for Vanessa. She was no longer at her assigned seat.

"I thought he was really nice," Jessica replied. "It was good to talk about something other than Emily or myself for a while."

Claude felt somebody tap him on the shoulder.

"Excuse me, sir," said a young waitress.

"What is it now?"

"I'm sorry to interrupt, but one of your guests is very sick. She wants to see you."

"Not now! Have you seen Vanessa Sharp, the woman in the white suit?"

"That's her. But her suit isn't white any more."

The waitress pointed to the lower deck. Claude's face fell as he saw Vanessa leaning over the balcony. She was vomiting profusely, her suit marked with a cocktail of regurgitated prawns and what looked like rice pudding. The smell, wafting upwards, made Jessica feel queasy.

"Oh dear. Maybe I shouldn't have sat her so close to the buffet."

*   *   *

'Bondi Pride' returned to Circular Quay three hours after it departed. Most journalists danced merrily onto the jetty, having overdosed on the free champagne and party atmosphere. Vanessa had to be carried off, though she conceded she was to blame and assured Claude she had had a wonderful time otherwise. Claude supplied her with a *Bondi Place* T-shirt and arranged to have her vomit-splattered suit dry-cleaned, earning him extra brownie points. Nesley, too, was full of praise for the event. She farewelled Blake with a peck on the cheek and reminded him of their date with the staple gun. All things considered, the outing had been a great success.

CHAPTER EIGHT

BONDI PLACE
BLOCK 6
Episodes 26–30

Synopsis:

Emily, Stefan and Racine decide to go camping for the weekend. Stefan doubts that Racine will survive a night in a tent and bets her one hundred dollars that she will pack her bags and return to the comfort of home within twenty-four hours. They borrow a four-wheel drive and make their way to Patterson's Ridge, a secluded spot in the bush with only a creek to wash and bathe in. Stefan is impressed by Emily's knowledge of bush survival techniques and their friendship develops. Meanwhile, Racine is pestered by mosquitos. After much sufferance she gives in and decides to stay at a nearby motel for the last night of the weekend. Stefan happily collects one hundred dollars for winning the bet. Racine decides to walk back to the main road but, as darkness begins to fall, she becomes lost and frightened. Back at the campsite, Stefan and Emily start a fire and toast marshmallows. Amid the romantic setting, they kiss . . .

Jessica and Holly had very different reactions to the latest batch of story-lines. Holly loved the idea of Racine getting lost in the bush and was already considering how to play the scenes. Jessica, however, couldn't even contemplate a rehearsal of her upcoming story.

"I can't do it!" she said. "I can't kiss him. They'll have to shoot it from behind or call in another stunt double – I can't kiss Blake on the lips!"

Holly was amused by Jessica's protestations. "I thought you two were getting along. When are you going to admit you're really stuck on him?"

"In his dreams!" Jessica insisted.

"Dreams are subconscious. How can you be sure you don't dream about him as well?" Holly asked with a mischievous grin.

Blake joined them in the Green Room. He was running late and had worked up a sweat in his mad rush to get to the studio. Jessica felt awkward when she saw him.

"Have they called me yet?" he asked urgently. No pleasantries, not even a smile. Just a bad mood and a bad hair style. He'd pedalled all the way on his push bike.

"They're running half an hour late. Sadie's wig has vanished so they have gone out to buy a new one," Jessica explained.

Blake moved over to his pigeon-hole. All the actors had a shelf where their scripts and fan mail were deposited, although neither Jessica, Blake nor Holly had received any letters yet.

"You'd better stop eating garlic," joked Holly as Blake picked up his script. "You'll soon be eating for two."

Jessica screwed up a piece of paper and threw it at Holly, as if to say, "Shut up!" Meanwhile, Blake picked up his script and read the first page of the synopsis which outlined the romantic development between Stefan and Emily. His face was expressionless.

"Maybe I should leave the two of you alone," Holly went on. "Let you get in some practice."

Still Blake didn't react. He was preoccupied – a neighbour had reported an argument with his father who had apparently been drunk at the time. Though the incident in itself was no big deal, it set off warning bells for Blake. He had seen very little of his father lately, but enough to detect that his drinking had escalated. Worried, he couldn't focus on anything else. He read the words on the script but they meant nothing to him.

"I'm going to get a bite to eat," he said, dumping the script back into his pigeon-hole. "If Gus calls me, tell him I won't be long."

He left the room. Jessica didn't know what to think. *Is he annoyed because he has to kiss me?* she wondered to herself. Holly observed her troubled thoughts.

"I know exactly what's going on in your mind," she said. "And you reckon you don't like him!" Jessica herself couldn't come up with any explanation for the way she was feeling.

"We're ready for Racine," said Gus as he popped his head through the door. This was Holly's cue that she was required on set.

"If I don't see you before, I'll see you tonight," she said to Jessica as she left for Studio Four.

Tonight? It took Jessica a full thirty seconds to remember what Holly was talking about. Tonight was the night *Bondi Place* hit the air.

* * *

The sun descended behind the Sydney Harbour Bridge, a silhouette of golden orange framed by the imposing arms of the famous structure. Holly marvelled at the breathtaking sight from the lower balcony of the Fairgate mansion.

"I can't believe you come home to this every night," she said to Jessica. "I had no idea you were this rich."

At first, Jessica hadn't realised it either. Up until the age of thirteen she believed everyone lived on the water and had a housekeeper who appeared twice a week. "Strange, isn't it?" Holly continued. "I'm playing the rich girl and you're playing the country bumpkin, when in real life the roles are completely reversed."

Jessica agreed it was rather ironic. "Do you miss your father?" she asked.

"Yeah. I phone him every couple of days but all we seem to do is fight. It's Auntie Agro's fault."

"You mean Auntie Agnes?"

"Yeah – I mean Auntie Agnes! Oh, I guess she's not that bad. It's just the generation gap, you know," said Holly with a giggle.

Jessica looked at the sunset. She always felt calm and serene at this time. Maybe it was because the setting sun forced her to reflect upon what had happened during the day.

"We're really lucky you know," she said. "Most girls would kill to be in our position. Do you ever think 'Why us?'"

"Ten times in the last thirty seconds, to be exact. But I don't like questions that pose more questions," replied Holly.

"Like what?" asked Jessica.

"How are we going to cope? What's it going to be like when everyone recognises us? What am I going to wear to the Oscars?"

Jessica laughed. "Do you ever worry that it will change you? This fame business?" she asked.

Holly gave careful consideration to her answer. "Already has. And I'm glad. I don't want to be the girl I was. The girl on the farm, the one with the mud on her face who spent all day dreaming but never doing. I want to be someone, and I think I will be."

Jessica appreciated the insight. She sensed that underneath Holly's confidence she lacked self-esteem and had suffered pain in the past. Jessica knew her mother had passed away some years ago and suspected this had something to do with it. Holly seemed determined to change. Fame seemed to have become her path to fulfilment.

"What about you?" Holly asked.

"I don't know. I tell myself not to get caught up in the hype of it all. Maybe it's a defence mechanism. In case it doesn't happen."

"That's silly," said Holly. "You've got it all. A great house, a great family. If I were you, nothing would stop me."

Jessica had heard Holly's observation from others many times before. But she didn't believe it. Now that the subject was focusing on her insecurity, she didn't want to talk any more.

"We'd better go inside," she said. "We're on in half an hour."

* * *

Meredith and Malcolm Fairgate always had a glass of wine in the formal living room after dinner. On this important occasion – the night their daughter Jessica made her debut on national television – another person was sharing their ritual. Auntie Agnes was tipsy after a second glass of red.

This was the first time the Fairgates and Auntie Agnes had met. They were from different ends of the social spectrum. Auntie Agnes was a grey haired, salt-of-the-earth type woman who knew more about life than facts and figures. Conversation was very hard to sustain.

"How are you all getting along?" Jessica asked as she and Holly entered.

"Fine, just fine," said Malcolm loosening his tie. He looked every inch the high-flying businessman with his expensive suit, receding hairline and pot belly. He turned to Holly who had sat down beside him. "So how does your father feel about you giving up full-time study?" he asked.

"He thinks it's great. He always encourages me to pursue my dreams. He knows this is a fantastic opportunity and is happy I'm keeping up with my studies part-time. It's not easy."

Holly's reply was confident and natural. Malcolm was hoping for a chance to restate his views on the value of education but realised Holly would give him a run for his money.

"Yes, well . . . I've got just enough time to go over some paperwork before the show starts. Give me a yell when you're on," he said as he left for the sanctity of his study.

"I'll put the kettle on," said Meredith.

"I'll help," insisted Auntie Agnes, following her out to the kitchen.

"Your parents are really nice," said Holly.

Jessica found her observation quite amusing. Holly obviously hadn't picked up on the underlying tension over her study.

"Yeah, they're not too bad," she said.

"Wonder what Blake's up to?" said Holly, changing the subject in a suggestive tone of voice.

"Probably the same thing as us. Waiting in front of the box," replied Jessica.

"Maybe we should invite him over? Might be nice to watch the first show go on air together."

Jessica knew Holly was goading her but for once she didn't mind. She hadn't stopped thinking about Blake since she had seen him in the Green Room that afternoon. The more she considered it, the stranger it seemed that he hadn't made some comment about the kissing scene. Even a crass remark would be more satisfying – at least it would have been a reaction.

"Let's give him a call," suggested Holly. "His number's on the filming schedule." Holly rifled through her bag and retrieved the schedule. Jessica's instincts told her inviting Blake over was a bad idea but for some inexplicable reason she felt like living a little dangerously.

"You do the talking," said Jessica, reaching for one of the many extensions around the house. Holly found the number and began dialling. Jessica watched Holly's face intently as she waited for someone to pick up the phone.

"Oh, hi – could I speak to Blake please?"

A few seconds later a shocked expression appeared on her face. She hung up without saying goodbye.

"What happened?" asked Jessica.

"Total weirdness. Some grumpy man answered – must be his father. He was really rude. It was like an argument was going on – I think Blake was shouting in the background. Then he hung up on me."

Jessica was intrigued and concerned. Holly dismissed the idea quickly. "Oh well, that means it's just you and I," she said, reaching for the remote control and switching it on to Channel Eleven. The six o'clock news was in progress.

"And we'll be back after this break," said the newsreader. The first commercial was a promotion for *Bondi Place*. Holly, Jessica and Blake featured prominently.

"That's us!" beamed Holly. "This is insane! We're on national TV!" She looked at her watch. "Thirteen minutes to go!"

But Jessica's mind was still on Blake. *What on earth was going on over there?*

* * *

There were no lights on in the Dexter house. Darkness was interrupted by filtered light from the street but this didn't help Blake in his search through the kitchen cupboards – a difficult task even with the best of lighting.

"Of all the nights for the electricity to be cut off. Why didn't you pay the bill, for crying out loud?" said Blake.

"I'm sorry," replied Eddie as he lit up a cigarette, providing a flare of light in the room for a moment.

"You could have told me you had a lighter!" said Blake furiously as he stumbled over to take it from him. "Here I am searching for a match to light the candles!" He lit one and propped it on the coffee table.

"Things have been a bit tough lately. You know, with finances," said Eddie.

"I told you I'd chip in," Blake reminded him.

"I don't need your money," Eddie insisted. "I'll pay the bill."

"Too late now. I was really looking forward to tonight. Just the two of us."

Eddie had been looking forward to it as well, much more than Blake realised. He had seen very little of his son since *Bondi Place* commenced production and missed the time they normally spent together.

"I bought a bottle for us, to celebrate," said Eddie. "It's in the fridge."

"You expect me to believe that?" Blake retorted. "I've seen the empty cans out the back. It's no wonder you can't pay the bills."

"I've got it under control," Eddie insisted, even

though he knew his problem was getting out of hand. "Now, do you want to have a drink to celebrate or not?"

"Celebrate what? The TV isn't working!" Blake paced backward and forward, fighting to keep his temper under control. "At least the phone is still connected. Who was it?"

"For you, I think. Couldn't see in the dark. I accidentally hung up."

The final straw. Blake grabbed his coat and headed out the front door.

"Where are you going?" asked Eddie. Blake replied by slamming the door firmly behind him.

Eddie punched his fist into the air. He had really spoiled things. He needed a drink.

* * *

Blake laid his coat down on the grass and sat down, doing his best to get comfortable. Misty clouds suffocated the glow of the moon, but it was just as well. Blake didn't want his next door neighbours to know that he was perched outside their living room, watching their television set through the lighted window. Nor did he want them to see the tear trickling from his eye. *Why is this happening again?* he asked himself over and over. Painful memories were floating around in his head – he saw his mother and father arguing, the sound of bottles breaking, his father crashed out on the floor. He thought that was in the past. Now, for reasons he didn't properly understand, his father was drinking as much as he ever did. His mother had left years ago as a result. Blake could only wonder: *What price this time?*

CHAPTER NINE

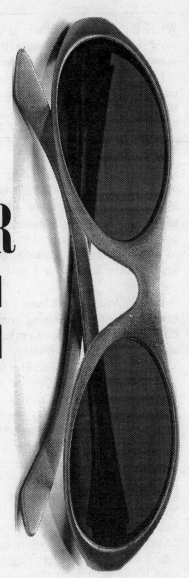

BONDI PLACE HITS A FIRST NIGHT LOW!

What do you have when you combine predictable plots, wobbly sets and appalling acting with a soundtrack of bop music? Answer: Channel Eleven's new soap, *Bondi Place*.

Last night's first episode dispelled the much-lauded theory that the standard of Australian television drama is improving. While our film makers achieve originality and innovation, our TV producers remain in the dark ages, with cliched story devices rampant with sexist and demeaning undertones.

From the very first scene – featuring Geraldo Mercardo and Sadie Palmer arguing over a hot dog on Bondi Beach – it was hard to tell if it was television drama, a half hour video clip or indeed a travelogue advertising the famous stretch of sand. Mercardo and Palmer are 'soap veterans' for a very good reason – neither has enough range or talent to advance to another medium. Indeed, the real life Bondi Beach life-savers, in the background, provided the best performances of the show.

Belinda Viola hasn't been seen on our screens since she quit her high profile hostessing role on the game show *Mystery Clue* three years ago to embark on an acting career. The reason for this is no mystery – when it comes to acting, Miss Viola doesn't have a clue. Her love scenes with Jared Hopper – who won a *Remote Control Award* last year for his role in *Pacific Place* – were as romantic as a block of wood. Comedian Rocket Rogers had the best line of the episode, rumoured to have been his own. "Somebody get me off this ship of fools!" he pleaded.

Newcomers Blake Dexter and Holly Harrison are obviously graduates from the modelling school of acting. Dexter's smouldering smile and Harrison's precocious pout punctuated their every line, their dialogue barely audible against the roar of the surf. Jessica Fairgate, another newcomer, showed the only glimmer of potential. With a little practice and a more flattering wardrobe she could become a star. If the show lasts that long.

— Jim Mapleton

The news rocketed through the Channel Eleven corridors faster than a speeding bullet. The secretaries in the typing pool were arguing about the implications; the tea ladies were gossiping in the cafeteria; even the security guards at the front gate were talking about it. Karen Wolfe was not amused.

"You are going to continue to hear a lot of rumours over the next twenty-four hours," she warned the assembled cast and crew in Studio Four. "I want to assure you there is nothing to worry about. It's early days. Every new show needs time to settle in and find an audience. I have no doubt that *Bondi Place* will do just that."

Karen was in damage control mode following the overnight ratings figures for the first episode. *Bondi Place* had, in the words of one of the many daily papers which offered scathing reviews, sunk like 'a ship of fools'. It was not good for morale.

"I'm going to leave you to it," said Karen. "The show must go on."

Karen left the studio. Michael instructed the gathering to take another five minutes to recharge their batteries. Blake drifted aside, a copy of the *Sydney*

Advertiser under his arm. The paper included an especially negative review of the show and, in particular, attacked Blake and Holly's performances. To Jessica's surprise, the critic said she had potential. She assumed Blake was upset about it and said consolingly: "Don't worry about it."

"About what?" replied Blake.

"The reviews. Critics don't know anything."

"Yeah, right," said Blake. He hadn't opened the paper and had no idea about the review. His thoughts were elsewhere. He and his father had argued again that morning.

Jessica felt for him. She was also troubled by the response Holly had received when she phoned the previous night.

"We phoned you last night to see if you wanted to come over and watch the show with us. Holly and her auntie were at my place."

"You did?" said Blake.

"Well, not me – Holly. She said some guy hung up on her."

Blake had no control over the nerve that snapped within him. The mere thought of Jessica and Holly – or anyone for that matter – learning about his father and their problems filled him with fury. He was embarrassed and ashamed and couldn't bear anyone to know.

"Don't ring me at home, okay?" he said sharply.

Jessica was taken aback. "Sorry. We were just . . . Since Holly and her aunt were over we thought maybe you and your dad . . ."

"Dad and I do our own thing, got it?" he said, his anger escalating. Jessica didn't know whether to be worried or angry.

"Look, this is pretty tough for all of us. You heard Karen. The show must go on. If you want, we can do some extra rehearsal . . ."

"Tough? You don't know the meaning of the word!"

Jessica didn't have to wonder any more: she was angry. Blake was like a tap running hot and cold. Before she could reply, Scott appeared with a pile of script amendments printed on pink paper.

"Good news, guys," he said dryly as he handed them a copy each. "Couldn't afford the bush, so you get to snog in the Surf Cafe. Tomorrow morning!"

Scott moved on to distribute the remaining scripts, leaving Jessica and Blake to ponder the next development. A cover note explained:

Due to a budget problem, next week's story-line involving the bush camping trip has been rewritten. The romantic development between Emily and Stefan will now take place in the current block of episodes, while the story involving Racine and Clarissa has been postponed to next week. All new scenes must be memorised overnight – Karen.

This was all too much for Blake. He cast the amendments aside and stormed out of the studio. Jessica shook her head with exasperation. This confirmed all her reservations about him. There was no point trying to help Blake – he didn't deserve it.

* * *

Holly wiped the tears from her eyes and looked in the mirror of the make-up room. *Am I really that bad an actress?* she thought to herself. *Does my voice truly sound like a cross between a chainsaw and a whoopee cushion?*

"Enough of that," said Lulu as she grabbed the tear-stained newspaper out of Holly's hand. "In times like these there's only one thing to do. A new hairdo is in order!"

"Not interrupting anything am I?" said the cheery voice of Claude, who had adopted an 'everything is wonderful' facade. "I've got a job for you, Holly. You're off to the fashion awards tomorrow night. You, Jessica and Blake are going to be in a celebrity parade."

Holly was confused. "But all the papers said I was terrible. How can they want me to be in a parade?"

"Listen, kid, the papers think everyone is terrible. They think Sadie is a shocker, Geraldo is a jerk. But those guys have been around for centuries – they've built careers on bad press. The public love it."

Holly considered this. It was true. Sadie and Geraldo were always criticised in the papers. Yet here they were on another show and they were popular. "I'll do it," she said.

Not that Claude was giving her a choice. "Good. Of course you'll be supplied with a dress to wear. I've also lined up an escort: Zac Winter!"

"Zac Winter!" exclaimed Holly. "I've been stalking him in the cafeteria for weeks. You mean I'm actually going on a 'date' with him?"

"Well, I wouldn't call it a date. The network bosses want their stars to arrive together. I've talked to Zac and he's cool about it."

"What did he say about me?" asked Holly.

"Nothing really," replied Claude. "He said he's seen you around."

He's seen me around! Holly's mind jumped into overdrive. She imagined photographs of them holding hands, articles in the papers and, of course, the big moment when they finally kissed.

"I'll have more details later on," Claude promised. "Talk to you then."

Claude shot Lulu a wink and left. Holly looked back into the mirror. Her tears were long gone.

"Zac Winter! Can you believe it?" Holly repeated to Lulu.

Lulu said nothing. She'd heard a few things about

Zac. One thing was certain – Holly would soon find them out.

* * *

Jessica was sitting alone at a table in the Channel Eleven cafeteria, surrounded by folders and textbooks. She gently massaged her temple. She felt like her head was about to explode. The fashion awards, lines to learn, school work to be done – it was all too much.

Blake watched her from a distance. He admired Jessica's dedication and wished that he, too, could be so studious. He found it hard enough coping with the *Bondi Place* workload, yet Jessica was also juggling school part-time. Considering his problems with his father, he decided they were probably under equal stress. With this in mind he tentatively approached her.

"You look like you could use a big slice of chocolate mud cake," he said.

Jessica regarded him warily. "No time for food," she replied.

Blake realised he'd have to work a little harder.

"Listen, I'm sorry about this morning. I've got a lot going on at the moment. I shouldn't have taken it out on you."

Jessica was surprised and touched by his apology. "Yeah, well, things can only get worse. I've read through the amendments. We've got a lot of work to do tomorrow."

Blake nodded. "You can count on me. I'll get my act together."

Jessica wasn't sure whether she should believe him. "Why don't you put your money where your mouth is? What are you doing tonight?"

Blake shrugged. "Nothing. Except learning my lines, that is."

"Then let's do some extra rehearsal of our own. I'll come over to your place . . ."

"No," said Blake firmly. "I mean . . . er . . . Dad's having a few friends over. I'll come to yours."

"Fair enough," said Jessica. "My address is on the schedule. Be there at eight."

* * *

Blake and Eddie sat at the kitchen table, which was littered with letters and bills. Blake nibbled at a take-away pizza as he sifted through the mountain of paperwork.

"I've paid the electricity bill, the phone bill and the rent for this week. I wish you'd told me about this sooner," said Blake.

"Didn't know how," admitted Eddie. "You're doing so well for yourself. You must be ashamed to have an old man who can't even hold down a job."

"Lots of people get made redundant," Blake assured him. "You'll get another job. What I'm worried about is this drinking. You've got to stop."

"I know. I will."

Blake desperately wanted to believe this. He looked at his watch. "I'm sorry, but I've got to go out again."

"But it's eight o'clock," Eddie pointed out.

"I know. Jessica and I have a difficult scene tomorrow morning. I'm going over to her place to do some rehearsal. I might be home pretty late."

Eddie was disappointed. Every time he had seen Blake in recent weeks he seemed to be running late for something.

"Will you be okay?" Blake asked.

Eddie realised that Blake was checking if he was able to stay away from the bottle.

"Yeah," he assured him. "Don't worry about me."

* * *

Blake and Jessica had read the revised dialogue four times. They were in the kitchen of the Fairgate house. As the scene was set in the Surf Cafe, they used the counter and table for props. Blake was surprised and impressed by the lavish surroundings, but was trying not to let on.

"Reckon I've memorised my half," he said. "Do you want to start doing the actions as well?"

"Guess so," replied Jessica. "But there's no need to rehearse the kiss," she added, unaware that she was blushing.

Blake, too, felt a little embarrassed. The thought of kissing Jessica was strangely awkward and exciting at the same time. "Good idea. Leave us something to look forward to."

Jessica's paranoia snapped into overdrive. *He's*

making fun of me, she thought. *If I were him I wouldn't want to kiss me. So why would he?* She quickly realised that she was babbling, and resolved to set it aside.

Meanwhile, Blake had been doing some thinking of his own. "Do you mind if I make a quick phone call?" he asked.

"Go ahead," Jessica replied. "I'll whip up some food. Do you like nachos?"

"My fave," said Blake.

Jessica handed Blake the cordless phone. He dialled his home number and waited.

At the Dexter house Eddie picked up the phone. An almost empty bottle of wine was in his other hand.

"Hello," he said, his voice slurring.

Blake realised his father was back on the bottle, and hung up immediately. "I have to go," he said to Jessica.

Jessica laughed. "You're joking, aren't you?"

Blake knew his behaviour looked bad and wished he could explain. But his father was more important.

"I'm sorry. This is an emergency. I'll go through the scene again on my own, promise."

A few seconds later he was out the door. Jessica was stunned – and furious.

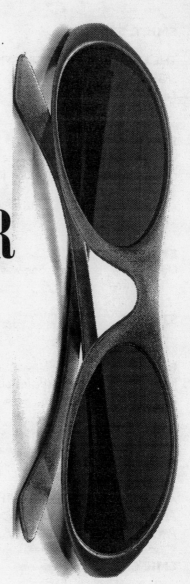

CHAPTER
TEN

SCENE 21.   INT. SURF CAFE   NIGHT

EMILY, STEFAN

THE SURF CAFE IS CLOSED. EMILY IS SITTING AT A TABLE, FIGHTING BACK THE TEARS. STEFAN OFFERS HER A BOX OF TISSUES.

STEFAN
C'mon. No need to cry. Racine will calm down by tomorrow morning. She'll give you your job back.

EMILY GRATEFULLY TAKES ONE OF THE TISSUES AND WIPES HER EYES.

EMILY
Don't know about that. She was pretty angry. Why has she got it in for me?

STEFAN
I think she's jealous.

EMILY
Jealous? Why would she be jealous of me? She's got money, she's beautiful . . .

STEFAN
So are you. You just don't wear as much make-up, that's all. But then, you don't need to.

ALTHOUGH TOUCHED BY STEFAN'S COMPLIMENT, EMILY'S LACK OF SELF-CONFIDENCE PREVENTS HER FROM TAKING HIM SERIOUSLY.

EMILY
You're just saying that.

STEFAN
No I'm not. That's why I think she fired you. Because she knows how I feel.

EMILY
I don't get it.

STEFAN
Racine's got a bit of a crush on me. Has for a long time. But I'm not interested.

EMILY
Really. Why not?

STEFAN LOOKS INTO EMILY'S EYES, SO BRIGHT AND INNOCENT. EMILY, TOO, NOTICES QUALITIES SHE HAS NEVER SEEN IN STEFAN UP UNTIL NOW.

STEFAN
I thought you would have worked that out by now.

STEFAN LEANS OVER AND GENTLY KISSES EMILY ON THE LIPS. EMILY IS SURPRISED AND EXCITED BY THE SENSATION.

EMILY
Stefan . . .

STEFAN PRESSES HIS FINGER ON HER LIPS.

STEFAN
Don't talk.

TAKING HIS FINGER AWAY, HE KISSES HER ONCE AGAIN, THIS TIME PASSIONATELY. FREEZE FRAME.

THIRD COMMERCIAL BREAK
END OF EPISODE

The first scene each morning is always difficult. Work begins early, usually by six am. The crew are still half asleep and the cast stiff with delivery of lines, so the process often takes longer than it should. This morning, an additional handicap was making the job even more time consuming.

"This is supposed to be a love scene," said Michael over a loudspeaker from the control room. "You kids are acting like two wet fish!"

The criticism was justified. Although Blake had memorised his lines, Jessica was still angry. Blake, too, was preoccupied with the situation he had discovered when he returned home the previous night. His father was rolling drunk. A raging argument had followed. He hadn't felt able to offer Jessica any explanation.

"Okay, let's take a break," Michael continued. "You two go and sort out your differences. We haven't got all day."

"Over here," Jessica suggested as she walked off the Surf Club set.

"Guess we'd better get it together," Blake said.

"What do you mean 'we'? You're the one who

disappeared last night. If you had stayed . . ."

"I know," Blake admitted. Before he could go any further, Claude bubbled onto the set.

"Sorry we're late," he announced as he entered the studio with Vanessa Sharp and a photographer from *Remote Control* magazine. "Where is our star couple?"

One of the cameramen directed them to Blake and Jessica.

Claude greeted them with a smile. "Morning kids. You remember Vanessa? She wrote that nice review of the show in last week's issue of *Remote Control*."

Blake and Jessica recognised Vanessa. She was one of the few journalists to write positive reviews of the show – even though she had been violently ill on the media cruise. Claude was treating her like royalty.

"She's come to do a story on the big scene."

A story?! Blake and Jessica were mortified. As if there wasn't enough pressure. On top of their personal embarrassment about the love scene, a journalist and photographer to watch meant an extra stressful ordeal. Claude's bright and happy facade was laced with a serious undercurrent. His smile belied the warning: "Don't stuff up!"

"Time's up," said Michael over the loudspeaker. Jessica and Blake made their way to the Surf Cafe set, followed by Claude, Vanessa and the photographer.

Jessica sat down at the table and Blake assumed his opening stance behind the counter where Stefan would collect the box of tissues.

"And action!"

Jessica and Blake launched into the scene. The dialogue flowed naturally until the moment when they were due to kiss. They looked into each other's eyes. For the first time ever, Blake felt in tune with Stefan. He could relate to what attracted Stefan to Emily as he could see similar qualities in Jessica: an honest, hard-working and dedicated soul. Jessica, too, felt a new appreciation for Blake. This performance proved he could be a competent actor when he tried. Blake leaned over and allowed his lips to gently touch Jessica's. He closed his eyes. Jessica, too, blocked out everything else. The sensation was brief but titillating. The world seemed to stand still yet the earth beneath them was moving.

"And cut!"

The crew erupted in a chorus of wolf whistles and applause. Blake and Jessica backed quickly away from each other. It was as if they'd both had an out-of-body experience. Before either could comprehend what was going on, Claude swooped in.

"We need you to do it one more time for the photographer," he said, practically pushing them back into tongue-diving position.

"We may even get the cover with this one," Vanessa enthused.

The magnitude of this was not lost on Blake or Jessica, or particularly Claude. A national magazine cover might just save the show.

* * *

The black stretch-limousine cruised down Darlinghurst Road in Sydney's notorious King's Cross district, the capital of sex and sin. Holly and Jessica sat in the back seat with their respective dates for the evening. Holly was paired with Zac Winter, and Jessica with another Channel Eleven celebrity named Sebastian Pope. The boys were wearing tuxedos and the girls glamorous gowns, organised by Leo.

"Isn't he gorgeous," Holly whispered to Jessica as

she wriggled closer to Zac. "I can't believe we're in a limo together."

"This is just like Las Vegas," commented Sebastian, revealing teeth stained by too many cigarettes. Jessica found him a total turn-off.

"Is Vegas a club?" asked Zac, who was wrestling with his bow tie.

"Don't you know anything?" laughed Sebastian. "It's the capital of America."

Jessica had thought Sebastian the more intelligent of the pair until that comment, which confirmed they were both as thick as two short planks. Holly, however, thought Zac was to-die-for. She was definitely in heaven.

"Do I look okay?" Holly asked for the third time in the last seven minutes. "You look like a lollipop," Zac replied, a lascivious glint in his eye.

"You don't scrub up badly," said Sebastian to Jessica.

Jessica shot him a sour look. She was loathe to say anything encouraging to either of the boys.

"Wonder who they got to be Blake's date?" Holly said.

Blake's name reminded Jessica of the love scene. She

desperately wanted to tell Holly about the sensation she'd felt but couldn't confide in front of the boys.

"Some Channel Eleven bimbo," she replied, hoping to sound nonchalant. Holly was too preoccupied with Zac's admiring eyes to continue with the subject.

The limousine finally turned into William Street, the busy motorway which connects the eastern Sydney suburbs to the city centre. A mobile phone rang. Zac and Sebastian both reached into their top pockets but the call wasn't for either of them. Holly reached into her tiny purse and retrieved her latest purchase.

"Holly Harrison," she said into the compact digital phone. She had bought it that afternoon in Double Bay and this was her very first call.

"Relax! We're on our way."

* * *

Claude had never been so relieved to see four people in his life. The minute Holly, Jessica, Zac and Sebastian stumbled into the backstage chaos of Sydney Town Hall, he grabbed them by the arm and whisked them off to their respective changing rooms.

"And don't fall over on the catwalk!" he instructed them.

The girls were overwhelmed by the dazzling event. After being photographed by dozens of paparazzi upon arrival, hassled for autographs by fans who knew their names, they were now about to turn models on a catwalk in front of a star-studded crowd and millions of television viewers.

"This is the craziest day of my life," Holly said as a young assistant helped her out of her dress. "Be careful not to rip it, whatever your name is. I have to return it tomorrow."

Jessica, too, was spinning out. She couldn't believe it was still the same day of her love scene with Blake. Glancing at her watch, she noted it was roughly twelve hours since her lips touched his. Looking through the half-open door of the changing room, she could see the door to the male quarters and wondered if Blake was behind it.

"Earth to Jessica," the assistant said as she clicked her fingers in front of Jessica's face. "We haven't got all night."

Jessica slipped out of her dress and squeezed into

the silver frock provided. The celebrity parade show-cased the most outrageous designs and both girls looked like aliens from a galaxy rampant with pre-dators – both gowns featured sharp spikes made out of lightweight metals sprouting in all directions. Jessica could hardly move.

There was no more time for discussion. A man burst through the door, completely oblivious to the fact that many of the girls were half-dressed.

"Listen up everyone," he said.

"Who are you?" asked Kimberley Turner, the cur-rent hostess of *Mystery Clue*. Jessica suddenly realised why Belinda had refused to do the parade – she and Kimberley were arch enemies. Kimberley was still in her bra and Holly took the opportunity to look closely to see if the rumours were true. To her disappoint-ment, she couldn't see any scars to indicate breast implants.

"I'm the director of this shambles," replied the man. "And I've got five minutes to transform you 'Muriels' into Cindy Crawfords!"

* * *

"And Holly is wearing . . . And Jessica is wearing . . ."

Holly and Jessica completed their round of the stage, a dizzying experience to say the least. Upon the futuristic set it was impossible to see anything. Laser beams flashed, special effects exploded out of nowhere and cameras swooped in and out to capture the action. Amazingly, nobody collided or tripped over and they both survived to tell the story backstage.

"Wow," said Holly. "We're lucky to be alive."

"So that's why models have to be two metres tall," Jessica decided as she kicked silver stilettos off her aching feet. "The brain mustn't register pain up there."

They rushed back to the dressing room, passing Zac, Sebastian and Blake on the way. The male celebrity parade was about to start. Responding to the theme 'Beachwear of the Future', the designs utilised lightweight material to provide protection from the sun. Blake was wearing a neck-to-knee swim-suit.

Blake and Jessica's eyes met for a second. He thought she looked like an astronaut from a space ship; the kind he wouldn't mind being on board.

Jessica had to admit to herself that he looked rather fetching as well. Not having time to acknowledge each other, both concluded they had been snubbed.

*   *   *

"Thanks for joining us. See you next year." The plastic hosts signalled the end to a plastic evening. As the credits rolled the plastic model paraded the winning dress. It was made of revolutionary plastic.

At long last the awards were over – but the real competition was just beginning. Three hundred people were pushing and shoving their way out of a single exit. Holly sadly observed that her favourite television stars could be just as rude and impatient as the worst yobbos at a footy match.

"Let's blow this fabric fiasco," said Zac. "We're meeting a few people down at Palpitations. Wanna come girls?"

Palpitations was a club on Sydney's notorious Oxford Street, the hub of night life and all things good, bad and ugly. Holly had heard a lot about it, especially among the crew and older cast members.

She had never been to a night club – the closest she'd ever come to one was a Blue Light Disco at the Ballina Bowling Alley.

"Do you wanna go?" she asked Jessica, nudging her to say yes.

Jessica was busy searching the crowd for Blake. She hadn't seen him since the parade and assumed his seat was somewhere else in the hall. She had, however, spotted his date – a Channel Eleven weather girl named Cynthia – chatting intimately to a fashion designer.

"Jessica! Do you want to go out or not?" Holly persisted.

Jessica now gave the question her full attention. "You must be kidding. We've got all that homework to do. I'm getting a cab home."

Besides, Jessica was not about to go anywhere with Zac or Sebastian. She didn't like the idea of Holly going either, but knowing Holly and not wanting to sound like Auntie Agnes, she refrained from giving unwanted advice. Holly was getting along well with the boys and probably wouldn't listen anyway.

The crowd became more hostile and Jessica and Holly

lost sight of each other. By the time they made it outside, Jessica felt like she'd been run over by a herd of elephants. She decided Holly would forgive her for taking advantage of the cab which appeared in front of her.

* * *

Holly, Zac and Sebastian waited fifteen minutes for Jessica.

"She's done the runner on you," Zac finally said. "We can't hang around all night. Palpitations will be going off by now. So what do you say?"

Holly was unsure. One look at Zac's dimples made up her mind. "Count me in. If I can get in, that is. I'm only fifteen."

"Fortunately you don't look a day under twenty-one. Leave it to me," Zac replied with a smile. A very dangerous smile.

* * *

"I think you know what this is all about," said Karen Wolfe, the fine lines around her eyes tight with anger.

"I'm deeply disappointed in you. Appearing at the fashion awards was a huge honour. Why did you have to spoil it by going to that dreadful club afterwards?"

Holly sunk further into the chair in Karen's office. "I didn't know the police were going to raid the joint. The bouncers shouldn't have let me in if there was risk of trouble," she replied weakly.

"You told them you were twenty-one years old! At least that's what I heard on the radio this morning."

Holly realised her defence was weak. She had made a terrible mistake in allowing Zac to talk her into going to Palpitations. Apart from the damage to her professional reputation, she felt personally betrayed as Zac had disappeared soon after their arrival at the club and Holly had seen nothing of him since.

"Have you nothing more to say for yourself?" Karen asked.

Holly burst into tears. She had not meant any of this to happen. It was as if her world had suddenly turned upside down and she had lost all control. Karen's anger subsided and her heart softened. The iron woman could be serious no longer. She had a soft spot for Holly and sensed the girl was out of her depth.

"Come on, no need to cry. As far as the night club incident goes, well, I'm sure we're all guilty of sneaking in underage at some time. The difference is you have a public profile to consider. I will overlook this as long as it doesn't happen again."

Holly wiped the tears from her eyes. "Promise."

"I'm afraid other people at the network are pretty angry about this as well. I'll try and calm them down. In the meantime, I suggest you keep a low profile. Do your job and do it well."

Holly appreciated the magnitude of the trouble she was in. "Thanks Karen," she said. "I won't let you down."

CHAPTER ELEVEN

MEMORANDUM

— CONFIDENTIAL —

TO: KAREN WOLFE

FROM: TOM DOYLE
            SCRIPT DEPARTMENT

RE: FORWARD PLANNING

Dear Kaz,

This is to confirm the items for discussion at our meeting this afternoon. Pretty drastic stuff, but I'm sure you'll agree it's necessary if we are to be really serious about improving ratings.

* Clarissa's triple heart bypass --- Sadie has real life heart problems as well --- good publicity angle

* Stavros declared bankrupt --- forced to sell Surf Cafe

* Stefan and Emily get married --- possibility of interstate location shoot for the honeymoon. How about Tasmania?

* Racine dies in car accident (at Sir Angus' request, remember?)

Rain was falling on *Bondi Place*. Torrential rain. The weather reflected the mood – the overnight ratings figures saw the show plummet to third spot in the six-thirty timeslot. It was quite embarrassing considering a cartoon re-run was among the opposition.

Jessica and Holly sat in the location van overlooking the beach. Michael had no choice but to halt filming, which gave everyone more time to dwell on their misery. Rumours were also circulating that major changes were afoot. More experienced cast and crew read between the lines. Their jobs were in danger.

"Zac hasn't returned any of my calls," moaned Holly. "I don't know. Why did he give me his number if he didn't want me to call?"

"He's bad news, Holly, take my word for it," Jessica replied.

"Why – you won't take my word about Blake," Holly pointed out. "Remember the way you were rambling about him backstage? And you look so cute on the cover."

Holly was referring to the latest issue of *Remote Control*. The photograph of Jessica and Blake kissing earned a small spot on the cover, overturning to a huge double page spread toward the back of the magazine.

"I suppose we do. The journalist . . . what'shername . . . Vanessa made a few bloopers with our quotes. She made it sound like I had a real life crush on Blake."

Holly shot Jessica a 'So, what else is new' look.

"Don't start on that again," said Jessica. "The fashion awards proved it. Blake didn't even say hello."

"Did you say hello to him?" Holly asked.

Jessica realised she had a point. "I guess neither of us really had a chance. I'm glad he's off sick so I don't have to see him for a while. I'm sure I'm reading more into it than is actually there."

"Maybe you should send him a sympathy card?" Holly suggested. "What exactly is wrong with him?"

"Food poisoning, I think," Jessica explained. "Apparently he ate something that didn't agree with him at the awards."

Scott appeared in a *Bondi Place* raincoat. He was carrying a huge bundle of scripts. "Hi groovers. More food for the workers," he said as he handed them the pink documents. "Blake has asked for two more days off so the writers have come up with some new scenes to replace the ones he was in. I'm afraid you two are in most of them."

"But what about Emily and Stefan? Something has to happen between them." Jessica pointed out.

Scott produced another pile of scenes and handed them to Jessica. "That's what these scenes are all about. You and Blake will have to do them when he gets back. That reminds me. You haven't spoken to him by any chance, have you?"

Jessica was surprised by the question. She never spoke to Blake outside work engagements, especially after he lost his temper when Holly phoned him at home. "You must be kidding," she said.

"Maybe you should," Scott suggested. "We've been sending all the scripts to his house but nobody has spoken to him to confirm he's reading them. It will be a nightmare if he doesn't know his lines when he gets back."

Jessica knew Scott was right. Despite her protestations, she was actually pleased to have a reason to contact him.

"I have the afternoon off so I'll get the cab to drop

by his place. I'll make sure he's doing his homework," she said.

There was a knock on the window of the van. It was Michael. He waved to Jessica to indicate they were ready to resume filming and she was required.

"Give Blake a big kiss for me," Holly suggested with a chuckle.

"Ha ha ha," said Jessica as she grabbed a raincoat and left for the beach.

* * *

Jessica had never been to the Sydney suburb of Randwick, even though it was on the same grid reference as her harbour-side home in the street directory. The taxi driver found Blake's street without difficulty but had trouble finding the house. Eventually they realised it was the only house in the street without a letterbox. There was, however, a utility van stacked with furniture in the driveway.

Jessica stepped out of the taxi and looked at the house, a 1950s-style weatherboard in very bad condition. She approached the front door, expecting Blake to be annoyed at her appearance, but determined to ensure that he learned his lines. She thought any argument would be between the two of them, so was surprised to hear a screaming match taking place through the open fly-screened door.

"You're nothing but an ungrateful no-hoper," she distinctly heard an older man say in a slightly slurred tone. He sounded a bit like one of the drunks Jessica sometimes heard down at her local mall.

She stepped onto the porch and accidentally kicked a beer can in her stride. The can rattled down the steps and the shouting stopped. By the time Blake appeared at the door Jessica had noticed dozens of other empty cans lying around.

"What are you doing here?" he said in a none-too-pleased tone of voice.

"I've come to make sure you received the revised scripts," she said. "Is everything okay?"

"Why shouldn't it be? You shouldn't have come."

"You shouldn't have said you had food poisoning. You look as fit as a fiddle to me."

Jessica's observation was true and it threw Blake completely. It was then that Eddie stumbled out.

"Who's this then?" he asked as he smiled at Jessica. "Wait a sec. You're the chick from the telly." Eddie patted Blake on the shoulder. "Aren't you gonna introduce your old man?"

Blake had never been more embarrassed in his life. Jessica, too, felt uncomfortable. She wasn't prepared for any of this. Her heart went out to Blake. She regarded Eddie with a kind smile.

"Pleased to meet you, Mr Dexter," she said.

"I'll learn my lines and be at work tomorrow. Good-bye, Jessica," said Blake. He was deeply ashamed that Jessica was seeing what was really going on in his life.

There was nothing left to say. Jessica turned around to face the empty street. She hadn't thought about how to get home but she knew it wasn't a good idea to stay. As she walked toward the street, Blake realised he'd been harsh. Too harsh.

"Jessica. Wait."

* * *

'BLAKE WOZ 'ERE '88'

Jessica read the graffiti on the park playground and

thought of a seven-year-old Blake etching his name into history. She could imagine him as a brat of a child.

"I used to kick the footy around here every day after school," Blake recalled as they walked around the small community park located at the end of his street. "The days I went to school, that is."

"How long has your father been an alcoholic?" Jessica asked tentatively.

"He drank a lot when I was a kid," Blake explained. "That's when Mum left. I thought he was okay until a few weeks ago. Bad has become worse pretty quickly."

"Why do you think that is?" she asked.

"I blame myself, more than anything," Blake admitted. "Dad just lost his job. I should be spending more time with him. He gets lonely."

"You never said anything. Maybe I would have understood . . ."

Blake finished her sentence. "Understood why I took off from your place that night? Why I did a runner after the awards? Why I had to say I was sick?"

Jessica nodded. "Maybe I could've helped."

"I don't want sympathy," Blake replied. "There's

more to Dad than the bottle. We do okay. We'll get over this. I just needed the time off to find somewhere permanent to live. Dad abused the real estate agents on the phone and they want us out. So do the neighbours. Reckon it's for the best."

By this time they were sitting at opposite ends of a rickety see-saw.

"So where are you going to go?" Jessica asked as her end went up into the air. Blake sank to the ground.

"I've lined up a flat. Should do for a while."

"Your father needs professional help."

"Try telling him that."

Jessica was enthralled by this new and unexpected insight into Blake. Her contempt for him had been replaced by admiration. She struggled to weigh down her end of the see-saw but Blake was too heavy. She wriggled forward in an attempt to bolster her end. Instead, she toppled head first toward Blake who caught her, preventing her from hitting the ground.

The sun came out for the first time that day. Blinded by the light, Jessica was paralysed in Blake's arms. He leaned closer. She covered the remaining distance.

They kissed. This time there was no script, they were not in a studio and there was no director to yell "Cut". The scene was very much for real.

* * *

Holly walked along the busy corridor of Channel Eleven toward the *Bondi Place* headquarters. Her mood was low and despondent. Everyone seemed to know about the night club incident and she could hear gossip and whispers from all directions.

"Hi, Holly," said Scott as he walked past carrying another bundle of script amendments. A green slip of paper dropped out from among them.

Holly kneeled down to pick it up and when she rose saw Zac approach from another corridor. Their eyes collided.

"Hi, Holly cake," he said.

Holly couldn't believe the smile on his face. "I've been trying to get in touch with you. Where did you disappear to at the club? Do you know the trouble you landed me in?"

"Hey – chill baby," said Zac. "Wolfe-breath is

always busting a blood vessel over something. She'll calm down."

Holly was incredulous. "How can you say that? You also left me in that club all on my own. I was freaking out!"

Zac wasn't at all concerned. "Don't know why. I had a great time. See you later."

Zac continued on his merry way. Holly was shocked and devastated. *How could he be so mean?* she thought. Glancing down at the piece of paper in her hand, the sight of the word 'CONFIDENTIAL' attracted her attention. Precisely thirty-six seconds later her eyes read over the last line of the memo.

They're writing me out of the show! she realised. *My life is over!*

PART TWO

For Cliff, Jackie, Jan and Karen

CHAPTER ONE

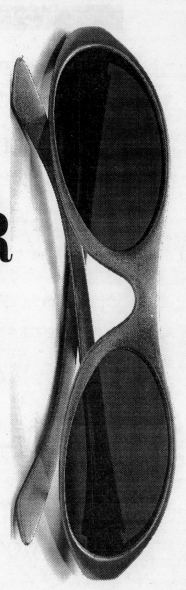

Meet the stars of

BONDI PLACE

Sadie Palmer
(who plays Stella Devereaux)

Holly Harrison
(who plays Racine Devereaux)

Blake Dexter
(who plays Stefan Elliott)

Jessica Fairgate
(who plays Emily Roberts)

AND

Belinda Viola
(who plays Maria Saint Peters)

Appearing
STAGE ONE
CHATSWOOD PLAZA

SATURDAY 10 AM

The white stretch limousine cruised down a tree-lined street in the Sydney suburb of Chatswood. The vehicle's mirrored windows reflected a clear fine day and deep blue sky. They also prevented curious onlookers from identifying its mysterious cargo. Slowing smoothly to a halt at a red traffic light, the car's back window slid open, as a mass of blonde hair escaped into the wind. Holly's face was clearly recognisable as she spat out her flavourless pink bubble gum.

"That's disgusting," observed Claude, the ever-nervous *Bondi Place* publicist who was sitting in the back seat opposite Holly and Jessica. "What if somebody recognised you? That's hardly proper behaviour for a star of *Bondi Place!*"

"Sorry," replied Holly, although it was clear that she couldn't care less. Her enthusiasm for her image and the show had died three days earlier when she had learned her character, Racine, was about to meet a violent end.

"That's not good enough!" Claude complained. "And look at your clothes. The public expect to meet

a glamorous television star. You look like an old pair
of socks!"

Holly knew this was true. She had woken up only
fifteen minutes before the limousine had arrived at her
home. As the driver honked the horn, she had a quick
shower, slipped into an unironed denim skirt and
recklessly applied make-up in record time. Jessica,
meanwhile, looked like a celebrity. Her hair and
make-up were flawless and her choice of a white
sleeveless dress perfect for the warm and sunny day.
And she had achieved it with minimal effort.

"I'm sure the public will be more interested in
everyone else," Holly replied. "They don't give a stuff
about me."

Claude's mobile telephone rang. As he answered it,
Jessica wriggled closer to Holly. "What's your problem?" she whispered. "You've been in this mood for
days. Of course the public are interested in you. What
makes you think the rest of us are more important?"

Because I'm about to be sacked! was on the tip of
Holly's tongue. She was tempted to confide in her
friend but pride prevented it. *How humiliating to be the*

first cast member to be sacked, she thought. And she didn't want to discuss it in front of Claude.

"I'm just in a shitty mood," she said. "Ignore me."

"How can I ignore you?" argued Jessica. "I'm your friend. I know something is wrong. A week ago you couldn't wait for this shopping centre appearance."

"That was before . . ." Holly stopped herself.

"Before what?" Jessica demanded.

Claude finished his phone call and looked over at the girls. He was smiling from ear to ear. "Great news. Our number one heart-throb can make it after all. He's over the food poisoning."

The thought of Blake stirred Jessica's feelings. Three days had passed since she had visited him at home – since she had had a go at him, since he had had a go at her and since their argument had dissolved into a kiss. Her lips tingled as she remembered. She felt nervous at the thought of seeing him again.

"Yeah . . . great news," she said.

Holly seized the opportunity to divert the subject from herself. "I still reckon there's something you're not telling us," she teased. "You two are made for each other."

Claude was excited by the hint of a real life romance. "Please," he wheedled. "Tell me you've got the hots for Blake. An on-screen/off-screen couple is just what we need! Think of the publicity!"

Jessica was surprised that the chemistry between them was so evident. "That's all in your imaginations," she insisted. "Blake and I are just friends."

Although her words were convincing, her thoughts were confused. She had considered little else since they'd kissed – how she felt about Blake, how he felt about her and whether a relationship was a possibility. She had concluded that she did like him but wasn't entirely convinced that he was serious about her. For this reason she'd resisted telling Holly about it. *After all, it's been three days and he hasn't phoned me*, she thought to herself. Phoning him had not entered her mind.

The limousine rounded a corner and a huge shopping complex appeared. Half the size of a football stadium, it housed four major supermarkets, two department stores and countless speciality shops. The car park was jam-packed.

"Show time!" beamed Claude. "We're meeting Terry Carmichael, the compere, on the top floor. He'll run through the schedule. It should all be pretty easy stuff. We're expecting at least two hundred people. So, whatever you do, don't get stage fright!"

Holly's stomach was knotted with butterflies. She couldn't decide whether to be excited about her first moment of public adulation or depressed because it might be her last. Catching a glimpse of herself in the driver's rear vision mirror, she suddenly realised the enormity of her dilemma. *I've dreamed about this for such a long time*, she mused. *So what if it doesn't last? All the more reason to enjoy it!*

Jessica squeezed Holly's hand, still deeply concerned for her friend. "We have to talk," she said. "I don't know what the problem is, but you must tell me."

But Holly adopted a cheerful and determined face. "I don't have a problem," she said. "Well, not today. Let's go and have a good time."

* * *

Stage One was located at the centre of Chatswood Plaza. Four levels of shopping overlooked the small arena, which was vacant except for a microphone and a few plastic chairs. An eye-catching sign screamed: 'MEET THE STARS OF *BONDI PLACE* TODAY 10 am'. A small crowd was beginning to gather.

Claude, Jessica and Holly entered through a back door on the upper level, which was where the most exclusive boutiques were located. A short, fat and balding man wearing a yellow striped suit and a red bow tie was awaiting them.

"Hello, hello, hello," he beamed. "Nice to see you, Claude."

Claude extended his hand. "I'd like you to meet Terry Carmichael," he said to Jessica and Holly. "He'll be introducing you on stage."

Jessica and Holly smiled and exchanged amused glances. Terry looked like a circus performer.

"You kids wouldn't be old enough to remember me," he bubbled. "I was on Channel Eleven the very first day it went on air. 1956 – had my own show. *Time for Terry* it was called."

"I've seen your portrait on the wall," said Holly.

Terry smiled proudly. "Really? Is it still in the foyer?"

"No – just outside the ladies' loo."

The veteran star was non-plussed. "That's management for you," he moaned. "Out with the old . . . in with the new."

"Any sign of Sadie and Belinda?" asked Claude, steering the conversation back to the task at hand. Sadie and Belinda were the only well-known *Bondi Place* stars who had agreed to appear. They had been chauffeured to Chatswood Plaza in a second limousine.

"They're waiting backstage," replied Terry. "Shall we join them?"

"Just a minute," said Claude. "We have to wait for Blake Dexter. You remember – the young man I told you couldn't make it. He's just phoned to say he's feeling better and can be here after all."

Jessica's eyes met Blake's as he made his way up the

escalator, wearing white jeans and a white T-shirt. He waved and smiled at the group. He was completely unaware that three eleven-year-old girls were hot on his heels.

Blake reached the top floor as all three girls caught up with their idol. They were waving autograph books but seemed more interested in smothering him than seeking a signature.

"Blake!" one of the girls screamed.

"I love you," gushed another.

The third girl was so starstruck she couldn't utter a word.

Claude rushed over. "Come on, girls," he said, sounding like a proud father. "Try not to kill him!"

Two security men appeared. "We'll take care of this," said one of them.

"Hold on," Blake insisted. "Let me sign their books first."

Jessica watched as Blake asked each of the girls their names, writing individual messages for them along with his autograph. One of the girls snuck a kiss onto his cheek.

"Don't miss the show," he said as the security men led them away.

"Glad you're feeling better," said Claude to Blake. "This is . . ."

"Pleased to meet you, Terry," said Blake smoothly. "I've seen your portrait around Channel Eleven."

Claude was impressed, even if Blake's reference to the portrait was now bittersweet. But Terry was charmed.

Blake's eyes drifted to meet Jessica's. She was trying desperately to appear nonchalant. They were nervous and excited to see each other again. But the time was not right to discuss feelings. Blake simply mouthed "Hello". Jessica responded with a smile.

"Now the family is together, let's head backstage," suggested Terry. "We'll take the staff elevator. That way Blake's fan club will leave us in peace!"

Terry led the way. Jessica and Blake drifted behind.

"Have you settled into your new place?" she asked.

"Sort of," Blake replied. "There's still a lot of unpacking to do. Thanks for keeping quiet about all this. I'd be in heaps of trouble if Karen found out I wasn't really sick."

"Let's just say you owe me one," Jessica suggested with a chuckle.

The group reached the elevator and squeezed inside. Jessica found herself pressed up against Blake. She didn't know that Blake could have easily taken a full step backward to make more room for them both.

*　*　*

A crowd of three hundred people waited: in front, above and even below Stage One. A burly security guard discovered two pimple-faced teenage boys lurking beneath the steps joining the stage to the dressing room, each with cameras poised to take shots of the *Bondi Place* stars from an angle never seen on television screens. The young offenders were quickly led away.

"I don't believe it," said Holly as she watched through a small opening in the backstage door.

"What's going on out there?" asked Jessica.

Holly opened the door a little wider to reveal the crowd in its entirety. Some had been waiting for several hours, having secured the best vantage points and stocked up with drinks and snacks.

"How can they say our show is a flop?" Holly observed. "Look at all these people. They wouldn't be here if they didn't like us."

The irony was not lost on her. Even when she thought about it objectively – which wasn't easy – she truly believed the producers were making the wrong decision in axing her character Racine.

"Attention, everyone," shouted Terry, trying to command the attention of the group in the backstage room. "We must do a quick rehearsal."

Jessica and Holly joined the group, which now included Sadie and Belinda. Sadie was typically over-dressed in a fluffy pink mohair jumper and a loud floral skirt, while Belinda was casually attired in a sleeveless black top and matching cotton flares. Sadie claimed to hate public appearances but actually re-velled in them. Belinda was genuinely scared of crowds

– so much so that she had quit her hostessing role on the game show *Mystery Clue* when its producers had decided to invite a studio audience.

"Okay, kiddies," Tony began, in much the same way he had opened his variety show back in the 1950s. "This is the deal. I go out first, tell a few jokes, warm up the crowd. Then I'll introduce you one by one. Beginning with . . ." he cast his eye over the group. "You, Belinda."

Belinda grimaced. "Please . . . not me first. I'd rather get lost in the middle."

"I don't mind going first," said Sadie, as if she was doing everyone a big favour. "I take it we're doing the usual – 'Hi, it's nice to be here, are you happy to be here? . . . I can't hear you!'"

Terry, however, was clearly tired of the same old thing. "I thought we'd try some improvisation."

Jessica, Blake, Holly and Belinda paled. *Improvisation?!* With only a few minutes before they were scheduled to appear, anything other than a basic routine seemed foolhardy and dangerous.

Sadie, however, liked the idea. More confident than

the others, she hoped this approach would favour her, making her more popular with the crowd. "Great. Just like in the old days!" she chuckled.

* * *

"So that's why I'm never getting married again!" Sadie concluded as the crowd clapped and cheered. "Four times is enough, don't you think?"

Terry laughed and nodded. Checking his watch, he realised Sadie's time was well and truly up. "Let's hear it for Sadie Palmer!" he said, stepping back to allow the soap opera queen to shine on centre stage.

Sadie basked in the attention, waving her hands and encouraging the crowd to cheer. "I love you all," she gushed.

"Thank you, Sadie," Terry continued, gesturing one of the stage hands to escort her away. Jessica, Holly and Blake watched anxiously through the small window in the backstage door, moving just in time for Sadie to burst through.

"They love me," she trumpeted. "Reckon I've earned a shopping spree. Help me with this, will you, Claude?"

Claude helped Sadie remove her red-blonde wig. With her naturally brown hair, a pair of glasses and a black jacket buttoned over her pink top, she looked totally different. "I'll be back for the finale," she promised on her way out.

"It will be our turn any second," Jessica said. "I'm terrified. What will he make us do?"

Holly, too, was having an uncharacteristic crisis of confidence. "We can't go out there and perform a comedy routine without a rehearsal!"

"Yeah, Claude," said Blake, looking at the publicist. "You said we'd only have to sign a few autographs. We're going to look like idiots."

"Sorry, guys. All Terry's idea," said Claude helplessly.

Belinda was looking increasingly queasy. Jessica noticed that her face was very pale.

"Are you okay?" she asked.

Belinda opened her mouth to speak but couldn't.

Blake and Claude could see she was on the verge of collapse and rushed to support her.

On stage, Terry adopted a deep voice to read from a tiny card with a question mark printed on the back of it. He was parodying *Mystery Clue* and its well-known host.

"Solve this mystery," he began. "I'm blonde, five foot eleven in height and incredibly gorgeous."

"Oh no," said Holly to Belinda. "Terry's introducing you."

Belinda felt even sicker. She thought Terry's impersonation in very poor taste. And she loathed any reference to her game show past. "I can't go out there," she said, covering her mouth and swallowing hard to prevent regurgitation of her breakfast.

Meanwhile, members of the audience began chanting. "Belinda! Belinda! Belinda!"

"Correct!" said Terry. "How about a round of applause for the lovely Belinda Viola!"

Cheers from the crowd, a deathly silence backstage.

Claude attempted to prop Belinda up. "Snap out of it, honey! You have to go out."

But Belinda wasn't going anywhere.

"Come on, Belinda. Don't be shy!" Terry continued with a wink to the audience. Although his tone of voice was light he was growing annoyed at what he had to assume was lack of professionalism backstage.

A few seconds later Blake dashed out.

Terry was shocked, but did his best to recover his composure. "Belinda!" he mumbled. "My, how you've changed!"

The audience didn't mind the substitution. Blake noticed a group of young girls in the front row clutching their hearts and staring dreamily up toward him. Although his ego was healthy, he was somewhat surprised by his effect on them.

"I'm afraid you haven't been watching *Bondi Place*, have you?" Blake scolded Terry as he snatched the microphone from him.

Terry was gobsmacked. *What is this kid doing to my routine?* he thought.

Blake walked over to a corner of the stage and kneeled down to one of the star-struck young girls. "I bet you watched the show last night," he said. "Maybe you can tell us what happened to Belinda's character Maria?"

The girl was so excited to be in Blake's close physical proximity that she could hardly speak. "Um . . . she disappeared," she whispered.

Jessica and Holly watched from backstage – intrigued and impressed by the way Blake was handling the potentially disastrous situation. Linking Belinda's absence from the stage to Maria's disappearance in the show was a stroke of genius.

Terry realised that if he didn't follow Blake's lead they would both look like idiots. "That's right," he said. "It's our job to find her."

The routine continued for the next twenty-five minutes with Blake and Terry suggesting several humorous scenarios for what might have happened to Maria. They also tested the audience by asking them to recount Maria's movements through previous episodes. Most people offered accurate recollections of the storyline, proving that despite low ratings, those watching were engrossed.

Backstage, Jessica, Holly and Claude remained by

Belinda's side. She was still feeling sick with nerves. While pleased by Blake's quick thinking, Jessica and Holly felt increasingly nervous. He would be a hard act to follow.

"Well, I think you'd better go and do some more private investigating," Terry suggested to Blake, winding up the segment. "Let us know if you find her."

Blake waved farewell to the crowd and disappeared backstage amid rapturous applause. Terry looked at his watch and realised that they had run close to the time allotted. After all, the event had been advertised as a brief autograph-signing session and his decision to turn it into a slapstick comedy revue had the potential to cost thousands if security guards were required to work overtime.

"How did I do?" Blake asked as he rejoined his anxious co-stars. Neither Jessica nor Holly had time to reply – Terry's voice signalled their turn to perform.

"Now, seeing you girls are close to fainting, I reckon we should wheel out some eye-candy for the boys," he said with a giggle.

Jessica loathed the sexist and demeaning introduction but had no means of protest. She took minor consolation from Terry's decision to invite them out together – they would at least have each other for support.

On stage, Jessica and Holly took turns with the audience. Jessica's nerves slowly evaporated as she appreciated how genuinely interested and excited people were by her presence. Holly too was determined to enjoy every second of her diminishing time in the spotlight.

"Seems I've been doing too much talking," said Terry, who was now looking a little past his used by date. "Would anyone in the audience like to ask these lovely young ladies some questions?"

A dozen hands shot up in the air. Terry walked to the right side of the stage and held the microphone down to an elderly lady.

"I have a question for Jessica," she said. "My grandson would be perfect for you. Would you like to meet him?"

Everybody laughed. Jessica was amused and embarrassed.

"Come on, Jess," said Terry as he held the microphone toward her. "Sounds like an offer you can't refuse. Unless, of course, you already have a boyfriend?"

Blake watched Jessica from his position backstage. He thought of the moment they had kissed, of the sensations he'd experienced with the touch and taste of her lips. He wondered if she was thinking about the same moment.

"Um . . . no, I don't have a boyfriend," she replied. "We work really long hours so it would be quite hard to see anyone outside the show."

"Aha . . . very interesting," Terry said in a titillating tone of voice. "Do I detect a hint of romance with someone on *Bondi Place*?"

Jessica struggled, but could not suppress her blush. Although Terry was only mucking around, she couldn't help thinking about Blake.

"We'll see," she replied simply, giving Blake the distinct impression she was referring to her feelings toward him.

Terry continued to probe the audience for questions. The following three were all directed at Jessica, compounding Holly's fears that she was unpopular and reminding her of her upcoming demise from the show. *How could I possibly think I could come out here and pretend everybody loved me?* she thought as Jessica responded to the audience. *Nobody is interested in me.*

Finally, a fifteen-year-old boy directed a question to her. "Racine is my favourite character," he began. "What would you like to see happen to her in future episodes, Holly?"

The question upset her. Although the attention felt good, it forced her to reflect on her shattered hopes for Racine. She had often imagined her character running the Bondi Beach Surf Club or, better still, an up-market fashion boutique and wearing all the designs. This was all too painful to reveal. By the same token, she could hardly divulge Racine's upcoming death in a car accident.

"I don't mind," she replied flatly. "I trust the writers. They know what's best."

* * *

The *Bondi Place* theme song kept the crowd occupied while Terry briefed his star attractions on the finale.

"Pretty easy stuff," he explained backstage. "I'll announce you one last time and let you take a bow. Then you need to hang around and sign autographs for a while."

"I can't stay very long," insisted Sadie, who was back under her wig and wearing the outfit she'd purchased while the others were on stage.

Claude nodded appreciatively. "That's okay, darling. Stay as long as you can."

"How about you, Belinda?" asked Terry. "At least come out for the finale. Pay off that disappearance sketch Blake and I cooked up."

Belinda was still concerned about facing the audience. However, her stomach had settled. "I need some thinking music," she replied sarcastically. "That's the way we'd do it on *Mystery Clue*."

* * *

"How about one final round of applause for the stars of *Bondi Place*?" cheered Terry, stepping back to allow the soap stars to command the stage on their own.

Blake, Jessica, Holly, Belinda and Sadie held hands to take a final bow. Jessica felt Blake gently squeeze her hand. She looked sideways at him. He smiled back. It was a very private moment in a very public environment.

The next half hour was organised chaos, with the crowd coming forward to request autographs and to have their photographs taken with the stars. The majority of requests were directed at Blake, who found himself kissed, cuddled and even groped by adoring young girls. One cheeky grandmother ambushed him with a smooch on the lips. Sadie was annoyed at being upstaged in the popularity stakes and made a discreet exit after signing just a few autographs. Belinda also left hastily.

Jessica and Blake were very much in tune, sharing glances which were enough to satisfy them, but subtle enough to escape the attention of Holly and the crowd. However, the way Holly was feeling, they could have eaten each other and she wouldn't have noticed. She couldn't help thinking of how she was about to lose everything just as she was beginning to enjoy it. Finally, the emotional whirlpool sucked her under.

"I'm sorry, everyone," she said. "I can't stay any longer."

Holly signed a final autograph and dashed backstage. Jessica was confused and worried by her behaviour. *Something is definitely wrong*, she decided. She signed two more autographs and followed her friend.

* * *

Holly sat with her head in her hands, unsuccessfully fighting back the tears. Jessica put an arm around her sympathetically.

"Whatever it is, you can tell me," she assured Holly. "Is it to do with Aunt Agnes? Your father?"

Holly's tears turned to sobs. Jessica feared the worst.

"Is it to do with Zac Winter?" she asked.

Zac's name prompted a wail from Holly. She looked up. "That's only part of it," she admitted.

Jessica suspected that Zac had made some kind of

sexual advance to Holly, possibly laced with a violent threat. Jessica had heard terrible stories about Zac since they had all attended the fashion awards and was angry at herself for not warning Holly about him.

"Listen, I don't know what the drama is about but I do know you liked Zac and things didn't quite work out the way you'd hoped. The best revenge for you is to put him behind you. You still have your friends, your job . . ."

"My job!" cried Holly, unable to withhold the painful truth any longer. "That's just it . . . I'm losing my job. They're going to kill Racine in a car accident."

Jessica was floored. "What? How do you know? Are you sure?"

The look on Holly's face convinced her that there was no doubt in her mind.

"My career is over, Jessica. Everything I ever wanted, all my dreams . . . smashed into tiny little pieces. My entire world is coming to an end. I just wish I could die."

Jessica took her friend into her arms. There was nothing more to say.

CHAPTER
TWO

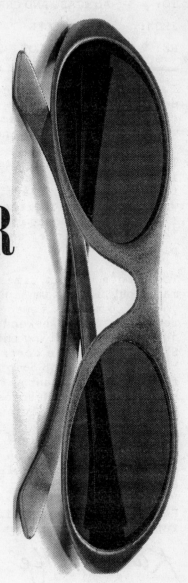

MEMORANDUM

TO: ALL CAST AND CREW

FROM: KAREN WOLFE

RE: NEW TIMESLOT

I am thrilled to announce that Channel Eleven has decided to reschedule *Bondi Place* from its current six-thirty timeslot to seven pm on week nights, beginning next Monday.

This can only be considered a positive step and an indication of the network's continuing support for the show's success. Our major competitor will be Channel Thirteen's *Mystery Clue* which I'm sure you'll agree is a tired and boring format (especially since our lovely Belinda departed!).

To promote the new timeslot, we are planning a major publicity campaign and we are counting on you all to make it a success. This means more interviews, more weekend appearances and more journalists visiting the set. In fact, Vanessa Sharp from *Remote Control* magazine will be in the studio today to compile a behind-the-scenes feature and will want to talk to as many cast members as possible. Needless to say, everyone must be on their best behaviour.

And a reminder -- the *Remote Control* Tenth Anniversary Party is on tomorrow evening. Make sure you get plenty of sleep tonight -- it will be a big one.

Rest assured, all this is very good news and our future is looking bright!

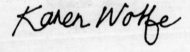

A sense of renewed hope and enthusiasm illuminated the *Bondi Place* Green Room as the memo
circulated. Unusually, most actors were present as
the scenes scheduled for filming featured a party
sequence involving all of the characters. Everyone
had something to say and it was difficult to get a
word in.

"I knew they'd switch timeslots," claimed Geraldo
as he lazed back in a chair, putting his feet up on the
coffee table. "The programmers were insane to think
that we could beat the Channel Thirteen news at six-
thirty."

Sadie, who was giving him a shoulder massage,
nodded appreciatively. "I'm sure we'll beat *Mystery
Clue*. What do you think, Belinda?"

Belinda seemed unhappy about the reference to her
past in the memo and was irritated by Sadie's quizzing
her about it. "I'm making a new rule," she declared.
"From now on, anyone who mentions my name and
Mystery Clue in the same sentence gets a punch in the
face!"

Everybody laughed, although Sadie realised that

she was deadly serious. Belinda was determined to be taken seriously and put her past behind her.

Rocket, who was most unpopular as a result of his snide remarks about the show, screwed up the memo and threw it in the bin. "Doesn't really matter to me," he scoffed. "I'm leaving as soon as my contract expires."

"Good," muttered Blake under his breath.

Jessica shot him a cheeky smile. Although they hadn't discussed their feelings, their words and body language indicated clearly that the attraction was mutual. Jessica felt inclined to talk about it, but, until the right moment could be found, she was content to allow things to bubble along.

The only cast member missing was Holly. But she soon drifted through the door, head low in line with the way she was feeling.

"Guess what, junior!" said Sadie, who enjoyed mothering her on-screen daughter, especially when she had an audience. "We're moving timeslots. Looks like all is not lost after all!"

Holly barely batted an eyelid. Jessica understood

her lack of interest – if she was being axed from the show, news like this would rub salt into her wounds.

"Over here, Holly," she said from her position on the floor. With all the cast in the room there were not enough seats to go around and, as Jessica, Blake and Holly were last in the pecking order, they had to settle for the carpeted floor.

Holly walked over and slumped down next to them. "I suppose I should say I'm very happy for you," she said quietly.

"You don't have to say anything," Jessica assured her. "How about we rehearse our lines?"

"What's the point?" Holly asked. "I'm on the first stretcher out of here."

Blake was confused but resisted the temptation to press for details. He had learned life in television was safer if he minded his own business.

At that moment, Gus, the assistant director, popped his head through the door. "Okay, people. Time to play. We need everyone except Holly and Sadie."

The actors and their respective egos began to file out the door, with Sadie blowing Geraldo a goofy kiss farewell. Her blatant flirting with him was obvious to everyone, except, it would seem, his after-hours fiancée. Their sudden engagement was still a major story in the tabloids.

"Sorry – I have to go," said Jessica apologetically. "I'll see you on set."

Holly smiled. Her horrific discovery had shown her what a genuine friend she had in Jessica. She wasn't sure what she would miss the most – Jessica's company or the fame and fortune she had dreamed that the show would deliver.

A few seconds later, Sadie and Holly found themselves alone in the room.

"Thank goodness we don't have to be in all those party scenes," said Sadie who, like Holly, had only to appear at the end of the sequence to bust the gathering the other characters were staging in their on-screen home. Glancing through her scripts for the week, Sadie made another interesting discovery. "Come to think of it – you're not in many scenes at all."

Holly was aware of this and had assumed the writers

were already edging her out of the limelight. Sadie sensed her disappointment.

"Are you okay, sweetie?" she asked. "You look a little pale. In fact, you weren't yourself at all during that dreadful shopping centre appearance on Saturday."

All of a sudden the pride which had prevented Holly from admitting to her fate dissolved, and she decided to tell Sadie the truth. After all, Sadie had become a mentor to her and she hoped to cement their relationship in her final weeks on the show. *I have to leave the show with one famous contact*, she had written in her diary the night before.

"Hold on to your wig," she began. "I'm being sacked from the show."

"What?!" replied Sadie, recoiling in horror.

"Racine is to be killed off in a car accident. I read it in a memo."

"Who else is in the car?"

"Huh?"

"Who else is in the accident? Am I in the car as well?"

Sadie's first priority was to establish whether or not she was also on her way out.

Holly was taken aback. "No . . . I mean, I don't think so. Er . . . wait a second. I read something about a heart condition."

Sadie put her hand to her heart, which was speeding into overdrive. She'd experienced this scenario many times before. Show plummets in ratings, major relaunch . . . cast members get the chop. She recognised all the warning signs and they were flashing.

"I have to call my agent. I'm sure there's a clause in my contract which says something to prevent this."

"But what am I going to do?" Holly pleaded, for the first time beginning to suspect what everyone else knew – Sadie looked after Sadie and any interest she took in Holly was purely for its novelty value.

Sadie paused. "Are you sure you read the memo properly?" she asked.

Holly nodded. "I think so. How can I find out for sure?"

"I'll teach you a little trick. Karen Wolfe is no mouse, but she's no monster either. If you are on a bus out of *Bondi Place* she'll probably wait until the last minute to tell you, so as not to upset your performance. However, by the same token, she's compassionate enough to stop you laying down your life on a future with the show."

"I don't get it," said Holly.

"Go to Karen and say you're thinking about taking out a loan to buy a house."

"But I'm only fifteen!"

"Okay – say you want to buy a car for that farmer father of yours. And say you'll need all the money you've got in the bank, plus a loan. Ask her advice."

"I still don't get it."

"If she says 'Go ahead' it means your future on the show is assured. If she says 'Best to wait', well, that's her way of telling you to make an appointment with the employment office."

The employment office?! Holly couldn't bear to think about it. She decided to act positive and to follow Sadie's advice, hoping that she had indeed misread the memo. Taking a deep breath, she left the Green Room on her mission.

Sadie promptly picked up her mobile phone and dialled.

"Yes . . . Sadie here . . . Sadie Palmer for goodness' sake! Is my darling agent there? I need to speak to him immediately!"

* * *

Karen Wolfe sat behind her desk, barely visible behind a mountain of scripts and paperwork. The producer looked much older than she had when production of *Bondi Place* commenced, less than two months earlier. A few grey hairs had infested her dark wavy hair, the wrinkles around her eyes seemed deeper, and her skin was dry and unhealthy-looking.

The other unwelcome addition to her face was a pair of red-rimmed glasses. Her eyes had been giving her trouble for months, but dedication to her work had taken precedence over a much needed follow-up visit to her optometrist. Removing the uncomfortable frames, she gently massaged her forehead: slow, circular motions eased but could not eliminate the hammer pounding inside her brain. New timeslot, new storylines, new publicity campaign . . . Sure, she had made it sound exciting in her memo. In reality, the entire prospect equalled a migraine.

"Excuse me, Karen," said Holly, who was standing tentatively at the door. "Have you got a moment to talk?"

Karen was pleased to see the young starlet. They had experienced a few ups and downs of late – notably when Holly was busted for partying under-age in a night club after attending the fashion awards on behalf of the network – but Karen could not hold a grudge against the naïve newcomer.

"Of course. What can I do for you?" she said.

Holly summoned all of her strength to suppress her anger. She played it cool and chose her words carefully.

"I'd like your advice," she began. "I'm thinking about buying a car for my dad. His birthday's coming up."

Karen felt flattered that Holly had chosen her for guidance on such an important matter.

"You see, I'd have to take out a loan," she continued. "It's a big step. I can probably afford the repayments on the money I'm earning now, but I'm just not sure it's a clever move."

Karen realised that Holly was fishing for reassurance about her future with the show. This was something Karen could not promise anyone – not Sadie, not Geraldo, not the biggest star in the universe.

"If I were you I'd hold off for a little while," she said. "That way you will be able to save for a bigger deposit and avoid forking out so much on interest. Yes, best to wait."

Best to wait! Sadie's exact words. Holly needed no more confirmation – Karen was saying her use-by date was up. Her body was trembling. *Why don't you cut the crap and come out and say it*? she muttered under her breath.

"Excuse me, Kaz," said Scott as he popped his head round the door. "Tom Doyle and the writers are waiting to see you."

This added insult to injury. Holly assumed that the meeting would involve discussion of Racine's car accident. She decided Karen was a very good actor – if it were not for Holly's inside information she would never have guessed.

"Gotta fly," said Karen. "Tom Doyle is a very impatient man."

Karen ushered Holly out of her office, locking the door firmly behind them.

Despite Holly's composure, her mind was running the gauntlet of emotions. Karen's denial was overpowered by hurt, hurt descended into anger. Finally, a dangerous frame of mind prevailed: revenge.

* * *

Vanessa Sharp sat in the shadows of Studio Four, battling the urge to fall asleep as she watched Jessica and Blake rehearse a scene. Claude tip-toed in to sit beside the *Remote Control* editor, armed with piping hot coffee. He had taken it upon himself to butter her up.

"I still find it exciting, even after all these years." He whispered so that his voice could not be heard on the sound monitor which was recording the scene. "The magic of making television!"

Vanessa turned up her nose. She had watched the filming of many shows and was very bored. "Yeah . . .?"

Jessica and Blake were oblivious to her presence. They were totally absorbed in the dynamics of the scene they were filming. Jessica, playing Emily, had just discovered that Blake's character Stefan was at risk of skin cancer. At the beginning of the scene, Stefan is reluctant to seek medical attention, but, in response to Emily's passionate pleas, finally agrees to visit a doctor.

Michael, the director, was impressed by their performances. He could see that both actors were in tune with their characters, but what he didn't understand was that they were playing the emotions for real. Jessica was considering the way she would feel if Blake was having a skin cancer scare and Blake, like Stefan, knew that he probably wouldn't seek help unless someone like Jessica encouraged him to do so. Such honesty in performance was rare and truly magical.

The three cameramen swung into position and Gus relayed Michael's "Action". The scene played to apparent perfection, so Jessica and Blake were surprised when Michael suggested another take. He requested a little more emotion from Jessica, suggesting Emily should go to the point of tears in her plea for Blake to see a doctor. Jessica responded, injecting so much desperation into her approach that it left her feeling physically and emotionally exhausted by the scene's end. Blake responded to her energy, prompting Michael to make an important mental observation: the key to extracting a better performance out of Blake seemed to be through Jessica.

With everyone satisfied, pages were flipped over to the next scene on the schedule. Stefan and Emily were again at the centre of the action with Holly's character Racine popping in to say two lines. Jessica was required to change her wardrobe and passed Holly on her way to the dressing room. They only had time for a quick "Hello".

Holly sat away from Blake on set. She was seething following her confrontation with Karen and needed to calm down before talking to anyone. Blake could see she was stewing over something and deliberately kept away.

At the other end of the studio, Michael and Gus were in deep discussion. A few minutes later Michael approached Holly.

"Good news, Possum," he began. "You can go and relax. We're cutting you from this scene."

Holly, however, was anything but pleased. "You're cutting me!" she fumed. "I spent ages rehearsing."

Michael was surprised by Holly's vehement reaction. Actors were usually thrilled to be removed from scenes as it made their workload easier. Ordinarily, Holly too would have been grateful but on this occasion linked it to her axing. She half-suspected Karen had instructed Michael to remove her from as many scenes as possible. *It's a conspiracy*, she decided. *They're probably laughing at me behind my back! Well, I'm going to have the last laugh!*

Holly stormed out of the studio, passing Vanessa and Claude on the way.

Claude attempted to make light of the incident. "Must be having a bad day," he laughed.

Vanessa responded with a smile, masking the most sinister of intentions. "I've just got to go to the bathroom," she claimed as she stood up to follow Holly. "I'll be back."

*   *   *

Holly sat on the kerb, her feet in the gutter of the road surrounding Studio Four. Her head was low. Vanessa took her by surprise as she sat down beside her and began to gently massage her shoulder.

"You're not having a good time of it at all, are you, sweetheart?" she said sympathetically.

Holly looked up, hurt and anger in her piercing blue eyes. "Is it that obvious?" she asked weakly.

Vanessa hesitated before continuing. Her next comment was a calculated guess – but well worth the risk. "They're axing you from the show, huh?"

Holly was stunned. "Yeah – how did you know?"

In a performance more convincing than any on the

Bondi Place set, Vanessa adopted a compassionate face and regarded Holly with maternal affection. "These things get around," she began. "Actors are always the last to know. It's terrible the way they all laugh about you behind your back."

Holly's worst nightmare was confirmed. *I was right*, she told herself. *It is a conspiracy! If Vanessa knows – everyone must know!*

Vanessa massaged Holly's shoulder a few more times, a gentle, soothing motion building to the ulti- mate stab in the back. "Cheer up. You still have the *Remote Control* party to look forward to tomorrow night," she assured her.

Holly forced a smile. All things considered, it was a minor consolation. "You still want to invite me, even though I won't be a star for much longer?" she asked.

"Absolutely," Vanessa assured her. "I'm going to look after you myself. And, sometime during the night, I suggest we have a little talk."

"A little talk?" Holly queried.

Claude appeared at the entrance to the Studio and

was soon on the approach. Vanessa realised she did not have time to elaborate.

"That's right. A little talk. A talk that will make you feel much better."

CHAPTER THREE

REMOTE
CONTROL

invites

the cast of
BONDI PLACE

to their Tenth Anniversary Party
at
the Ritz Carlton Hotel
Double Bay

Friday, February 12
7.30 pm

The golden invitation lay on the floor in Blake's new bedroom. A small, dark and damp space off the kitchen in the small apartment, the room was otherwise empty. He couldn't squeeze his bed through the door. For the last couple of nights he'd slept in the lounge along with most of the other furniture from the old house, all yet to be arranged.

"Hey, Dad – have you seen my black leather jacket?" he asked as he picked up the all-important card and walked through the kitchen to the living area.

"I think it's in one of those," replied Eddie Dexter, pointing at a stack of unopened boxes.

Blake rifled through one and discovered – to his surprise – that his father was right. The jacket needed a clean but was good enough to wear to the *Remote Control* party. Blake wanted to look his best, but not to the extent of finding a clothes brush to remove the dust. That would require far too much effort.

"What are you up to tonight?" he asked his father.

Despite the upheaval in their lives, the pair had been getting along well. Being responsible for their eviction from their previous place, Eddie was on his best behaviour and hadn't touched alcohol for almost two days.

"Got myself a date, haven't I?" he replied proudly.

Blake was stunned. "A date?! Where from?"

"Spotted her down at the dole office. We're having a feed tonight."

Blake was pleased – not only had his father resumed a social life but he'd been to Social Security, presumably to sort out the problem with his benefits. Clearly, the new apartment was inspiring positive resolutions.

"What about you?" Eddie asked. "Reckon you're pretty keen about that Jessica girl."

This put a smile on Blake's face. "I'd say things are going well for both of us," he replied.

"So are you two a couple, then?" Eddie persisted with a chuckle.

Blake screwed up his face. "That's so outdated, Dad! We're just chilling out, waiting to see what happens."

Eddie put his feet up on the coffee table, a wry look

on his face. "I see. Too chicken to talk about it," he observed.

Although Blake wasn't in the habit of discussing his relationships with his father, this attitude was uncharacteristic. "Since when have you been the 'Let's talk about our feelings' type?" he asked.

Eddie smiled proudly. "Meet the new me," he declared. "Sensitive New Age Man. Figure that's what's gone wrong with my love life in the past – from now on it's all out in the open. If I were you I'd take my advice!"

Blake laughed and tossed a cushion at Eddie.

Later, while he was blow-drying his hair, Eddie's words kept ringing in his head. *Maybe I should talk to Jessica*, he thought. The more he considered it, the more worried he became. *We haven't talked about how we feel. What if she isn't interested?*

His mind was made up. *Tonight's the night*, he decided. *We're going to sort this out. Are we a couple or not?*

He gargled half a bottle of mouth wash, hoping the outcome would mean that he and Jessica would end up in a position which would prevent them from talking altogether.

* * *

The classic black Rolls Royce ground to a halt in the Double Bay street, directly in front of Jessica's family home. Blake stepped out, looking every inch the television superstar in black satin trousers, leather jacket and ruffle-necked white shirt.

"I'll be back in a moment," he assured the chauffeur, a grey-haired man with a plum English accent.

"Take your time, Sir," the driver assured him, turning up the classical music while he waited.

Blake approached the front step, dodging the overflowing native ferns and creepers which lined the floodlit path. As he rang the doorbell, he found himself remembering the first and last time he had visited Jessica at home. Three weeks had passed since then. She had invited him over to rehearse a scene to be shot early the following day. The evening had proceeded well until Blake phoned home to discover his father back on the bottle. His speedy departure had infuriated Jessica.

In the moments before the door opened, he thought of how much had changed since that night. Jessica had discovered his father's alcoholism and proved sympathetic and supportive. The kiss which followed had been neither properly acknowledged nor discussed. *Tonight is the night*, he reminded himself.

The door opened. Blake did an immediate double-take – the attractive, flame-haired woman smiling at him was an older version of Jessica. The resemblance was uncanny.

"Hello," said Meredith Fairgate. "You must be Blake – although you're wearing more clothes than you usually do on television."

Blake laughed at the reference to his Speedo-clad character. "And you must be Mrs Fairgate," he deduced.

"Yes, but I'm better known as Meredith," she replied, extending a welcoming hand.

Blake entered the house to be greeted by the sight of Jessica descending the staircase. Images from old

Hollywood movies filled his mind – glamorous leading ladies in expensive jewels and designer gowns. Jessica had watched the same movies in awe and hoped to emulate the same legendary stars. Judging by the look on Blake's face, she had succeeded. Her choice of a lavender strapless ball gown could not have been more appealing to his eye.

"Hi, Blake," she said through her rose-painted lips. "Are you ready to go?"

Blake flashed his most debonair smile. "The Rolls is waiting."

"You two have a fun night," said Meredith. "And don't be late."

"Nice to meet you Mrs . . . er, Meredith," said Blake.

"See you later, Mum," called Jessica.

Walking back down the path toward the Rolls Royce, Blake felt like he was escorting Jessica on a first date. The fact that Claude had arranged for the pair to travel together stole nothing from the romantic atmosphere.

Blake opened the car door. "After you," he said.

Jessica stepped in and waited nervously for Blake to join her from the other side of the car. She could feel her legs covered in goose bumps and was grateful that her gown concealed them. *I've got to act cool*, she told herself.

Blake settled down beside her and the luxury vehicle took off smoothly. Jessica expected Blake to break the silence with a typically light-hearted remark, but he was too busy trying to formulate the right words in his head to actually say anything.

Jessica finally summoned the courage to speak. "Do you realise this is the first moment we've really had alone together since . . . well . . . that day?"

Blake was relieved. "I was thinking the same thing, but didn't know how to say it," he admitted.

The first big step had passed.

Jessica decided to bite the bullet. "So – what do you reckon?" she asked.

"About us?" Blake asked.

Jessica nodded. But Blake realised that the chauffeur was listening and had a wide grin on his face. Blake was annoyed – and a little embarrassed.

"Hey – stick to the road," he said, peering over the seat to give the eavesdropper a firm tap on the shoulder.

Jessica was amused. Blake, however, was completely thrown. He decided the time and place was wrong for this kind of discussion.

"We'll talk about this later," he suggested. Jessica wasn't sure if this was a good or bad sign. *Maybe Blake is waiting for a more romantic setting to tell me how much he cares about me*, she thought. At least, that's what she was hoping.

* * *

The Ritz Carlton Hotel in Double Bay was one of Sydney's finest, located in the heart of the exclusive suburb. A hint of salt air wafted through the hallowed halls which were only a short distance from Sydney Harbour. *Remote Control* magazine had spared no expense, hiring the lavish ballroom to celebrate their tenth year of publication. They were also determined to exploit the occasion from every photographic angle.

"Over here, Jessica," said one of the paparazzi.

"Give us a smile, Blake," screamed another.

"Let's have one of you two together," begged a third.

Blake and Jessica, who had just stepped out of the hired limousine, edged closer together. They looked every inch the couple.

Claude gently nudged the stiff-necked Blake. "Put your arm around her," he insisted. "And smile! This isn't a funeral!"

Blake obeyed the command. Jessica had a minute to enjoy the touch of his hand before Claude hurried them in the direction of the door.

A couple of screaming fans called out to Blake as he passed. "We love you!"

But there was no time to stop and talk – another limousine was on its way.

Holly looked through the window of the vehicle as it ground to a halt at the crowded entrance. She could see Claude and the photographers as well as a swarm of other celebrities mingling inside the foyer. This was undoubtedly the most star-studded event to which she had been invited. She knew too that it might be her last.

"I'm so sick of all this," moaned Belinda, who was sitting in the back seat with her. "They have this stupid party every year. I usually manage to skip it, but this time Claude wouldn't take no for an answer. It's just one long photo session, and everyone gets drunk in the process. Anything to save the show."

Holly rolled her eyes. *Why should I bother trying to save the show?* she asked herself. *It's not like they're doing* me *any favours!* Then, remembering Vanessa's kind offer to "look after her", she adopted a more positive frame of mind.

A male model dressed in a tuxedo opened the door to the limousine and extended his hand to Holly. Peering in, Claude was most unimpressed to see she was wearing a low cut red cocktail dress with a hole cut out of the front of it to expose her abdomen. He thought it looked tacky and highly inappropriate for this occasion. Regardless, the photographers loved it and snapped madly away.

As Belinda and Holly posed, Vanessa Sharp

emerged from the hotel. Holly waved and smiled. Vanessa appeared to return the smile, but, on closer inspection, it was actually a dangerous smirk.

The cat was about to eat the canary.

* * *

There was something slightly unnatural about the waiting staff buzzing around the banquet hall. For starters, they were all incredibly attractive. Secondly, none of them seemed to possess any hospitality skills whatsoever. This was confirmed when a perky young blonde spilt a tray of drinks over Jessica.

"I'm terribly, terribly sorry," the waitress gushed, with the sincerity of an alley cat. "Lucky that dress isn't see-through."

Jessica was prepared to forgive and forget until she took a closer look at the girl. She was distinctly familiar, although it took Jessica a few minutes to put a name to the blonde hair and exposed curves.

Finally, she remembered. "Samantha! Samantha Murdoch, isn't it?"

The girl gave a sly nod. Jessica and Samantha had crossed paths during auditions for *Bondi Place*. Samantha was an absolute bitch and Jessica suspected that she had doused her with drinks on purpose.

"I didn't know you worked here," said Jessica.

"I don't," Samantha replied. "The agency sent us. This isn't really my thing, but they're paying us fifty bucks an hour! Suckers."

Jessica could tell that Samantha was embarrassed and trying to justify herself. But Jessica didn't care that Samantha was waiting tables to make ends meet. As an actor, she knew she too might have to rough it one day, so thought no less of anyone doing it now. Samantha was the one with the problem.

"Nice to see you again," she said with a polite smile. "Don't worry about the champagne, either. I'm sure it will come out in the wash."

"I wasn't worried!" Samantha barked before turning sharply on her heel and heading to the other side of the room.

Holly grabbed the only surviving glass of champagne from her tray as she approached Jessica. "Hi, stranger," she said.

"Hi, Holly," Jessica replied. "You look hot!"

"I know!" said Holly shamelessly.

Jessica could tell her co-star was already tipsy and assumed she was trying to drown her sorrows. "How are you? I mean, really?" she asked.

Holly knew Jessica was referring to her termination from the show. Thanks to her third glass of champagne, Holly was dealing with her devastation quite well.

"I'm looking on the bright side. At least I'll be able to move out of Auntie Agro's," she replied, her speech slurring. "Well, I was going to have to anyway. She's practically packed my bags!"

Jessica could see through Holly's bravado but played along all the same. "Are you going home to Ballina?"

"Get real! I spoke to Darren this afternoon. He reckons he can get me heaps of work in Sydney. Top agent, that Darren."

Holly took another swig of champagne. At that

moment Zac Winter and Sebastian Pope – also known as the 'terrible twosome' – arrived. The Channel Eleven 'bratpackers' were a little wary of talking to the girls. They were well aware that Jessica didn't like them and Holly had landed in huge trouble after they'd talked her into a nightclub. This didn't stop them from sashaying over.

"Hi, babe," said Zac before giving Holly a peck on the cheek. "I'm pleased to see Wolfe-breath hasn't grounded you."

Jessica half-expected Holly to punch Zac in the face, but she was calm and collected.

"Nice to see you, too, Zac," Holly replied coolly.

Sebastian extended his hand to Jessica. "Hello, Miss Fairgate," he said in a pompous accent.

Jessica screwed up her nose. "Hello, Mr Dope. Er, sorry, Mr Pope."

Sebastian kissed Jessica's hand, leaving a puddle of saliva, which she wiped back on to his tuxedo. Innocent enough, except that Blake was watching quietly from another side of the room. His nose was a little out of joint.

Jessica's eyes collided with Blake's. He turned away, convinced he had misread the scene and had nothing to worry about. Jessica, too, worried for a second about how Blake might interpret what he'd seen. She dismissed it with amusement. *Paranoia or what?* she told herself. *We haven't even discussed our relationship. It's far too early to think about jealousy!*

One thing Jessica was definitely worried about was Holly. By this time she and Zac were deep in conversation of a very shallow nature. Jessica took Holly aside for a second.

"Are you okay?" she asked. "He's not giving you a hard time, is he?"

"I'm fine," Holly assured her. "All under control."

Jessica could sense trouble looming but knew better than to try to coax Holly away. She decided to go for a walk and find Blake. *Time to have that talk*, she decided.

"Catch up with you later," she said to Holly.

But Holly's ear was pressed to Zac's whisper and she didn't hear. Jessica quickly turned away. *If Holly's dumb enough to be sweet-talked by that loser I'm not going to hang around and watch*, she decided.

Circling the room, every second face was a famous one. Actors, talk show hosts, pop singers and even cartoon characters – all greeting each other with false affection, sometimes as a way of portraying power but mostly as a means of sucking up. This was one lesson about the industry Jessica had already learned – it pays to have everyone on your side. You could never know how someone might be able to help you in the future. She felt sorry for the actor forced to wear the Koala King animal suit, designed to represent the animated favourite. The room was stuffy enough as it was – experiencing it inside a furry koala costume must have been absolutely unbearable. She hoped they were being well paid for their discomfort.

Camera flashbulbs fired every step of the way.

To her disappointment, she couldn't see Blake anywhere.

* * *

Blake was no longer in the banquet room. Instead, he was half-naked in a hotel suite with the one and only

Samantha Murdoch. The aspiring actress had put on quite a performance to get him there – deliberately spilling a glass of red wine over his shirt, insisting he take it off and leading him, via the lift, to a suite to get stain-removing soda water from the bar fridge. Of course, the scene was not complete until Samantha attempted to seduce him.

"Whoa. Slow down," Blake insisted.

"What's wrong?" asked Samantha. "I thought this was what you wanted."

Blake had done nothing to give Samantha this impression, although in his usual circumstances it wouldn't really have mattered. The encounter was a fantasy come true – a mysterious and attractive girl comes on to him without warning, leads him to a hotel room . . . But there was no way he could go through with it. He couldn't stop thinking about Jessica. He couldn't afford – nor did he want – to jeopardise their blossoming relationship.

"I'm sorry," he said apologetically. "I think you're a little mixed up. I've got to get back to the party."

Samantha was taken aback. "There's no one better

out there," she boasted. "Especially not that cow Jessica Fairgate. I don't know how you can possibly work with her."

His sweetheart's name was all Blake needed to speed his departure – and compound his guilt.

"Why don't you go after Geraldo Mercardo?" he suggested. "He's more your type."

Samantha simply shrugged and tossed him his shirt. She wasn't the kind of girl to crumble in the face of rejection. *You've got to be in it to win it,* was her resounding motto. *And this turkey has just lost.*

* * *

Jessica imagined the 1970s had been exciting but couldn't understand the effect Abba classics had on survivors of the period. Geraldo was doing his best John Travolta impression on the dance floor, Sadie was trying to recapture her early days as a go-go dancer and even Karen was tapping her foot on the sidelines. Jessica figured they'd all smoked too much marijuana in their heyday and had suffered brain damage. Not a pretty sight.

"Let's lose it," said Holly as she stumbled into Jessica's line of sight. Zac, equally intoxicated, was by her side.

"Not in these heels," said Jessica, even though her shoes were quite comfortable. Truth was she would never have danced in front of a crowd, and certainly not to this music. She was far too self-conscious.

Holly and Zac disappeared on to the dance floor. Carmel Butter, the much respected reader of the rival Channel Thirteen news, was not impressed when Holly elbowed the back of her head. Holly didn't feel a thing, despite the fact that Carmel had so much hairspray in her black mop that it was like concrete.

Jessica watched Holly, unsure whether to laugh or cry. Others were watching, too. Although mortified by the spectacle, Karen and Claude knew better than to try to stop the girl. A scene would ensue, providing the scandal-hungry *Remote Control* journalists with material for their tabloid headlines.

Luckily the press hounds didn't notice Blake and Samantha's reappearance. A scandalous conclusion could have been easily drawn: Blake's hair was ruffled, his shirt hastily buttoned back on and Samantha looked like she'd just done an aerobics class. Fortunately, none of the journalists paid any attention as the two actors descended the elegant staircase. Unfortunately, Jessica had a full view. She was shocked, angry, and most of all, deeply hurt.

Holly's head was spinning. After five glasses of champagne she was off her face and bumping into everybody in her wake. Zac, who had stopped after four beers, was sobering up. He managed to grab Holly by the hand, spin her around and lure her into a dip. Holly felt like she was on a roller-coaster, stirring incoherent memories of days at the Ballina Fair where she'd thrown up over school friends and innocent onlookers. This time around it was slightly worse. As Zac lifted Holly back to her feet, her stomach gave way and a wave of vomit catapulted into the air. Carmel Butter chose the wrong time to open her mouth to speak.

Holly dashed to the bathroom; Jessica dashed home; and Blake was left wandering the room on his own.

* * *

Holly flushed the toilet, hopefully for the fourth and final time. She watched the water fill the bowl and settle to a calm, pristine blue. *Just like me – all washed up*, she thought to herself. It was as if the events of the last few days were hitting her all at once. There was a knock on the cubicle door. Holly's time was up – in more ways than one.

She summoned the strength to rise from the floor. Her dress was covered in stains from other people's drinks. She imagined that they, too, would discover stains on their clothes – and send her the dry cleaning bill. Fortunately, when it came to Carmel Butter, her memory wasn't as good.

Opening the door, she was greeted by Vanessa Sharp. Her smile seemed warm and sympathetic, disguising an ulterior motive.

"Hello, dear," said Vanessa. "Are you okay?"

Holly wiped the tears from her eyes. Removing her hand from her mouth, she attempted to speak but felt an after-shock of sickness rising from the pit of her stomach. She restrained it with her hand and burst into tears.

"Why don't we get you up to a room so you can lie down," suggested Vanessa. "When you're feeling a little better we'll talk."

Holly nodded.

"I'll just touch up my face while we're here," the journalist added. "You take a second to get yourself together."

Vanessa walked over to the mirror and opened up her handbag. As she reached for her lipstick, she retrieved a small tape recorder from a side pocket and checked the batteries. To her delight, they were fully charged.

* * *

The stars presided brightly over Sydney Harbour. The moon was almost full, casting a smoky blue light over melancholy waters. Boats bobbed up and down, houses were speckled over the distant shore and the occasional cheer of a midnight reveller wafted through the air. A tear trickled down Jessica's cheek as she absorbed the scene from the balcony of her home.

"Is that you, Jessica?" said a voice from behind her.

Jessica wiped her tears away, but it was no use. By the time her mother appeared at her side, another waterfall was on its way.

"What's wrong?" asked Meredith. "I didn't hear the car drop you off."

There was good reason for this. After witnessing the aftermath of Blake and Samantha's escapades, Jessica had left the hotel and walked all the way home. She knew better than to tell her mother this particular part of the story.

"I've made such a fool of myself," she admitted despairingly.

Meredith put a comforting arm around her. "What are you talking about?"

"Blake," replied Jessica. "I thought he . . ."

She allowed her words to trail off, feeling awkward about telling her mother the embarrassing details of her languishing love life. Meredith, however, didn't need to know any more. She remembered what it had been like to be Jessica's age and in love – the trouble she had gone to to impress a boy, the way she had asked her own mother how she looked a thousand times before stepping outside, the butterflies she had felt in the presence of that special person. Meredith recognised all of these things in Jessica's own behaviour. She guessed the night hadn't worked out with Blake.

"There, there," she said soothingly, taking Jessica in her arms and gently rubbing her back. "Let it all out."

Jessica cried like she had never cried before.

* * *

Blake fumbled with his keys at the front door of his apartment. There was no outside light so he couldn't see a thing. Leaning up against the door to regain his balance, he discovered it was open as he almost fell through it.

"Dad?" he called, thinking his father had come home and carelessly forgotten to lock the door behind him.

Switching on the light, however, Blake saw Eddie, passed out on the couch with an almost empty bottle of Scotch at his side. The picture was all too familiar.

"What happened to your date?" he whispered, trying to nudge his father awake.

Eddie barely stirred. "Over," was all Blake could understand from his slurred speech.

Blake slumped beside him on the couch. He knew that there was no point getting angry. His night had been bad enough. After surviving his encounter with Samantha, he had looked everywhere for Jessica but couldn't find her. He feared that she might have been sweet-talked by Sebastian Pope. *After all, I did see them fooling around together. He kissed her hand!*

Dismissing this wild assumption, he worried that she had gone cold on him. *Perhaps I was too slow in telling her how I feel?* he thought. *What a night!*

"Goodnight, Dad," he said, curling up next to his father. "Looks like neither of us had a very good evening."

CHAPTER FOUR

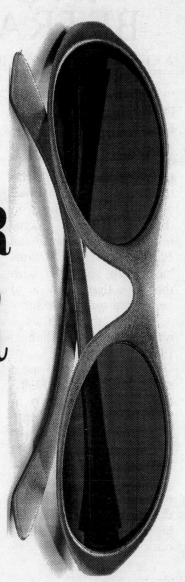

"I'VE BEEN BETRAYED!"

AXED *BONDI PLACE* BEAUTY SPEAKS OUT!

"I've been betrayed. I feel like I've been stabbed in the back!"

These are the words of an emotional Holly Harrison, the blonde bombshell who thought her dreams had come true when she won the role of bitchy Racine in the struggling soap *Bondi Place*. Now those dreams have been shattered with the news that Holly is to be written out of the show – without so much as a warning from the Channel Eleven bosses!

"Nobody has told me a thing," explains Holly, fighting back the tears at the *Remote Control* Tenth Anniversary party. "I had to find out by accident. I feel totally humiliated."

Despite the shock, fifteen-year-old Holly admits that in many ways she's looking forward to getting out.

"The show is a shambles. The story-lines are getting more and more ridiculous. Nobody tells you anything – you have to work it out for yourself," she reveals.

Falling ratings have also affected cast morale, according to the girl who hails from coastal Ballina. "Everyone is really depressed. There could be more cast changes."

Holly couldn't reveal how Racine is to be written out of the show but says it's a typical soap opera twist. "I was hoping for something challenging, maybe a disease. They've taken the easy way out."

Meanwhile, on a more positive note, Holly confirms rumours that co-stars Jessica Fairgate and Blake Dexter are a hot new item. "Didn't you know?" she asks. "I thought it was old news!"

— VANESSA SHARP

The staff at *Remote Control* magazine worked furiously over the weekend, fighting the tightest deadline
in their ten-year history. The glamorous birthday bash
had taken place on Friday night with all photographs
and interviews to be processed and ready for the
printers by Sunday afternoon. The new issue had to
be on the stands by the following Monday morning.

"Absolutely brilliant," cheered a tired but satisfied
Vanessa Sharp as the issue rolled off the press late at
eleven pm Sunday night. "I have a feeling this is going
to be our biggest selling issue yet!"

* * *

Jessica almost tripped over the copies of *Remote
Control* sitting on the floor of the Channel Eleven
foyer. The screaming headline threw her even more off
balance: '*BONDI PLACE* BEAUTY SLAMS SOAP!'
earned a small spot on the cover, accompanied by a
picture of Holly holding a glass of champagne. Below,
an even more startling headline and photo. 'PLUS,
HOT NEW ROMANCE!' complete with the shot of

Blake with his arm around Jessica, taken on their arrival at the party.

Jessica picked up a copy and flipped over to the invasive pages. *How on earth did this happen?* she wondered.

* * *

Holly held her head high as she walked through the *Bondi Place* headquarters in the direction of Karen Wolfe's office. She could feel all eyes upon her. No doubt everyone knew about her tipsy antics at the *Remote Control* party and were expecting fireworks from her confrontation with Karen. Holly didn't care. *It's not as if she can threaten to sack me*, she reminded herself. Little did Holly know, the stares and whispers were about a more serious development.

Karen was winding up a heated telephone call when Holly entered her office and nonchalantly took a seat. "That's right, no comment," she concluded as she slammed down the phone.

"Morning, Kaz," bubbled Holly.

Karen looked like thunder. Evidently she was not having a good morning.

"Is anything wrong?" Holly asked. She knew something was up but foolishly underestimated its seriousness.

Karen tossed her a copy of the red hot issue of *Remote Control*. Glancing at the magazine's cover, Holly felt the same sickening sensation that had consumed her just before she had thrown up all over Carmel Butter at the party. This was news to her.

"Oh God!" was all she could gasp.

Karen was incredulous. "Why, Holly? Why?"

Holly was struggling to come to terms with what she saw in front of her. She vaguely remembered talking to Vanessa Sharp but had never expected her drunken and emotional outburst to end up in print. She tore through the issue as she looked for the article.

"I don't understand," Karen continued. "What made you think we were writing you out of the show?"

Holly finally found the correct page. "I've been betrayed," she read, quoting the headline which quoted her. She couldn't recall using those words, ever.

"No – *Bondi Place* has been betrayed," Karen replied angrily.

By this time Holly was getting a grip on the situation. Though the article was a shock, her impending termination from the show had exhausted her thoughts. She had rehearsed this confrontation many times. She took a deep breath and spoke with confidence and conviction.

"I thought you would have had the decency to warn me," she began. "Finding out like that, well . . . it was terrible."

"What was terrible?" Karen replied with genuine bemusement.

"I saw a memo that said Racine was to be killed off in a car accident. I know everything."

The pieces suddenly fell into place for Karen. She was relieved but the situation had imposed an even greater problem.

"You silly, silly girl," she said. "Haven't you ever heard of a near-death experience?"

Holly looked blank. "Sort of."

"Well, that's what we had planned for Racine. She's

involved in a car accident and is pronounced clinically dead. We have a dream sequence and then she wakes up."

Holly was overcome with relief. "That's great! So I'm not to be axed after all! Forget everything I said, okay?"

Karen's expression told a different story. "I'm afraid it's not that easy. I had Sir Angus Beazel on the phone this morning. This article reflects very badly on the show and the network."

Karen paused for a quick mental scan of her vocabulary. But there were no gentle words to break the news. She had no option but to simply say it.

"In light of this incident, I'm afraid we're going to have to let you go."

* * *

Blake sat in the publicity office, the *Remote Control* issue in his hand. His reaction was divided – while he was thrilled everyone would know he and Jessica were an item, he hadn't actually seen or spoken to her since the beginning of the party on Friday night. He was worried that something had happened, something which might have affected their relationship.

"This stuff about you and Jess is wonderful," said Claude as he returned to his desk. "After the disaster with Holly, I'm relieved some good press came out of Friday night."

"Guess so," replied Blake.

Claude picked up on his reservations. "Listen, mate, I know you and Jessica have a certain . . . shall I say, chemistry? Holly's not the only person around here to interpret it as lust. You guys are the only ones who know the real story."

Blake assumed Claude was attempting to elicit the lowdown from him. This was something he could not give without talking to Jessica. "I can't really say," he replied.

Claude nodded appreciatively. "Fine by me. I'm not going to pressure you into anything. That is, on a private level. Publicly, however . . ."

"What are you getting at?" Blake asked.

Claude paused for a moment, searching for the right

words to express what he knew was a delicate proposition. "Let's just say the press love a real life soap couple. And, as I'm sure you know, what the press actually print and reality are often two very different things."

Blake struggled to make sense of Claude's round-about explanation. "Could you be a little more straightforward?" he asked.

"Fine," Claude replied. "I want you and Jessica to play the couple – for appearance's sake – regardless of what the truth is. That way the show gets good press and you guys boost your profiles, maybe even make some extra cash."

"Extra cash?" Blake queried, his eyes lighting up.

"That's right," Claude replied. "Magazines often pay for stories involving star couples – you know, 'A Weekend With . . .' And – dare I mention it – there's always money to be made out of a break-up."

Blake was loathe to consider that possibility, but the rest was appealing. Although he couldn't say for sure, he was reasonably confident all was well with Jessica and his affection for her was reciprocated. There

seemed no concrete reason not to go along with
Claude's plan.

"Sounds good," he agreed.

* * *

Holly entered the Channel Eleven canteen, prompting
a Chinese whisper to circulate the room within seconds.

"There she is," said the morning weather girl.

"Who?" replied an unshaven cameraman who was
chatting her up. "Hey – you mean the little bitch who
rubbished the network!"

"I've heard she's pregnant by Zac Winter," added
someone else. Minutes later, the story was entirely out
of hand and Holly was being described as everything
from a calculating vixen to a dangerous psychopath.

Holly didn't care about the snide remarks and icy
stares that followed her around the room – she was
worried about only one person. Finally, she discovered
Jessica sitting at a table with Lulu the make-up artist.

Lulu, now sporting green hair, almost choked on

her celery stick when Holly approached. "Here comes trouble," she warned.

Jessica looked up and regarded Holly with bewilderment. Although concerned about Holly's reported comments – especially as they involved her relationship with Blake – she was certain that there had to be some vaguely plausible explanation.

"I'd better make like the road runner," said Lulu, acknowledging Holly with an awkward smile. "See you both later."

"I wouldn't blame you if you told me to get lost," said Holly to Jessica.

"I'd prefer you to start talking," Jessica replied.

Holly sat down, fighting to keep a lid on her emotions. "I didn't say anything to Vanessa about you and Blake," she began. "How could I? I don't know if there *is* anything going on."

Jessica was inclined to believe Holly on this score. She hadn't told Holly about the developments with Blake, simply because she worried that her good news might have made Holly feel even worse in the light of her dismissal.

"Looks like Vanessa has done quite a hatchet job on you," Jessica replied sympathetically. "Problem is, you were drunk – there's not much you can say in your defence as most people will suspect you simply can't remember."

Holly knew this was true. "I know I said a few stupid things but I didn't expect them to end up in print. I hope I haven't ruined anything between you and Blake. I really believe you guys would be great together."

Jessica sighed, thinking of the incident she had witnessed between Blake and Samantha at the *Remote Control* party. "I haven't seen him all day. Don't worry about it – if things don't happen between us, it won't be your fault."

This came as quite a relief to Holly. "Well, I hope they do . . . happen, that is."

Jessica hesitated before asking the question on the lips of everyone in the room. "So . . . what did Karen have to say about all this?"

Holly was past the point of crying when it came to her future on the show. "That's the most ironic thing of all. You're never going to believe it."

Holly proceeded to tell Jessica about the entire misunderstanding – how Racine wasn't to be killed off, but because she had mouthed off about the show she had been handed a real death sentence. She was right – Jessica couldn't believe it.

* * *

Rocket Rogers sat in the Green Room in stitches of laughter. "I've been betrayed!" he said in a mock, whimpering, Holly-like tone of voice.

Jessica entered in time to witness his cruel impersonation. "Don't you have any compassion at all?" she asked the stand-up comedian, who was counting down the last days of his contract with the show.

Rocket was taken aback. "My goodness. The redhead has a temper!" he quipped, inciting Jessica's rage even more. "I'd better be careful what I say or your new boyfriend will come after me!"

Jessica was tempted to have a go at Rocket but thought better of it. He simply wasn't worth the energy. She was more interested in talking to Blake. The "are-we-or-aren't-we?" question had troubled her for long enough and she wanted some answers – beginning with exactly what had happened between him and Samantha.

"Have you seen him?" Jessica asked Rocket in her politest voice.

"They swapped some scenes around," he replied. "I think he's on location." Rocket checked his watch and realised that he was running late. "I'm supposed to be in the studio. Don't miss me too much."

Rocket disappeared in the direction of the studio, colliding with Claude on his way.

Spotting Jessica, the publicist's face lit up. "Hello, Princess," he gushed. "Love the story!"

Jessica realised that she had better set Claude straight. "Yeah . . . I need to talk to you about that. Thing is, Vanessa jumped the gun. Blake and I, well . . . um . . ." She hesitated, unable to find words to adequately describe the situation.

"Don't worry about that," Claude assured her. "I spoke to Blake this morning. He's agreed to play the loving couple, at least for appearance's sake. He knows the publicity is valuable."

Jessica grappled with what Claude was saying.

"What do you mean?"

"I told him about the money you two can make – selling stories on your private life, that kind of thing. You don't have to be a couple all the time – just when the press is around."

Claude's pager began to beep. He checked the message and realised that he was supposed to be elsewhere. "Gotta fly," he said.

Jessica was in a state of shock. A picture was beginning to form. *So Blake's only interest in me is publicity!* she concluded. Looking over at the table, she spotted a copy of *Remote Control* open to the page of the article. Rocket must have been reading it.

"How could you do this to me?" she said aloud to Blake's photograph. She thought of Samantha. If Blake was using her for publicity, it was also highly likely that he had been up to no good with the wannabe actress. *I feel like such a fool*, she said to herself.

Suddenly, there was no doubt in her mind that Blake had been using her all along.

*   *   *

Bondi Beach was a myriad of colour, chaos and collision. The brilliant blue sky was dotted with brightly decorated kites of all descriptions, dancing merrily in the breeze, while their operators tripped over each other on the sand. A major competition was in progress, providing plenty of entertainment for onlookers – and a nightmare for the cast and crew of *Bondi Place*.

"I can't believe Karen didn't know about this festival," Michael complained. "We could have scheduled these scenes for another day."

While the sight of dozens of kites had the potential to look fantastic on screen, the scene in question required the beach to be almost deserted. According to the script, Blake's character, Stefan, is bitten by a blue-ringed octopus and he collapses on the sand. His screams are supposed to go unheard – quite unrealistic with hundreds of people visible in the background. To make matters worse, most onlookers were more interested in the film crew than the kite show and were staring directly at the camera.

"What are we going to do?" Blake asked Michael. "If you want my opinion, we should drop the story altogether. Two weeks ago, Stefan thought he had skin cancer, now he's about to be bitten by a poisonous sea creature! Don't you think the scripts are getting a little out of hand?"

Michael agreed with Blake's sentiments. In response to the poor ratings, the script writers had hit the panic button. Story-lines were becoming increasingly ridiculous. Stefan was not the only character to ride the rollercoaster of dramatic story-lines. Sadie's character Clarissa had a heart attack one week, and lost her memory the next. Belinda's character Maria was kidnapped and then suspected of murder, all within one episode. The show was speeding out of control.

The director finally made a decision. "I'd better give Karen a call."

As Blake and the crew waited, a Channel Eleven car

parked illegally on the street nearby. Scott, the runner, was visible behind the wheel. Jessica stepped out of the passenger seat. She was in full make-up and costume to film the next scene, where her character Emily discovers Stefan unconscious on the sand.

As Blake and Jessica's eyes met, however, the thoughts behind them couldn't have been more different.

Jessica approached Gus, avoiding further eye contact with Blake. "Are you ready for my scene?" she asked.

"We're having a slight delay," Blake answered, forcing Jessica to look at him. "So, how are you?" he continued.

"Fine, thanks," Jessica replied icily.

Blake was taken aback by her coldness. "Are you sure? You sound a little, well . . . upset."

Jessica realised she would have to offer some explanation. "I was a little confused," she replied. "But I've worked it out now."

Blake was totally disoriented. *What has got into her?* he thought.

Michael ended his phone conversation with Karen.

"Pack it up," he instructed the crew. "There's no point shooting here today. We'll have to come back tomorrow."

The crew began to collect their gear, hoping that they would be given the remainder of the afternoon off. Jessica turned to walk back to the car.

"Wait!" shouted Blake.

Jessica backtracked and looked at him blankly. "Yes?"

"Do you want to go for a walk?" he began. "I really think we should have that talk. You know, the one I said we would have at the party."

Jessica was amazed by his cheek. *He's only trying to go along with his little plan!* she thought. However, she was tempted to take up the offer. On one hand she was eager to fire at Blake with both barrels – to confront him about his dalliance with Samantha at the party and more importantly, to expose his plan to use their relationship for his own publicity gain. On second thoughts, she decided that was not such a good idea – they would still have to work together and any further conflict was bound to impair their performances.

Better to end it quickly and easily, she decided. *This is painful enough as it is – I don't want my work to suffer.*

"We have nothing to talk about," she replied.

Blake watched her turn to walk toward the car. "Jessica!" he pleaded.

But she kept on walking.

Blake was mystified. Only one thing seemed certain – their relationship was over before it had had a chance to begin.

A little further down the beach, a brightly decorated kite swept high into the sky. Blake watched as a sharp gust of wind came from behind, breaking it in two and sending it, with a crashing finale, to the ground. He felt exactly the same way.

CHAPTER FIVE

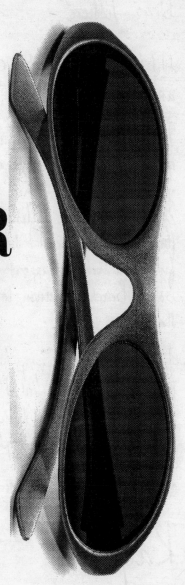

Dear Jessica,

Hi! My name is Ralph. You don't know me but I am your biggest fan!

I've watched Bondi Place since the very first episode and reckon it is unreal, mostly because of you. I don't care what the papers say! I think Emily is far more realistic than the other characters (but don't tell them I said that!). I can't wait to find out what happens next. Does she stay at Bondi Beach or return to the country? I hope she stays.

I know you are very busy and probably receive thousands of letters, but I would really love to hear from you. Even if it's just a few words or, even better, an autographed photo!

Hopelessly devoted to you (ha ha),

Ralph

Jessica couldn't resist a chuckle as she folded the letter back into the handmade envelope, lovingly decorated with drawings of hearts and flowers. *Hopelessly devoted? He doesn't even know me!* she thought to herself.

The *Bondi Place* Green Room was more crowded than usual, with Sadie and Jared attempting to rehearse lines in one corner and Belinda talking animatedly to a reporter on the phone in another. A couple of non-speaking extras – actors employed to appear in the background of scenes – were also lounging around. The roar of the newly installed cappuccino machine added to the noise. On top of all this, the television set was playing a forthcoming but unedited episode of *Bondi Place*, which had just been rushed from the studio. A scene featuring Stefan and Emily was currently on the screen.

Glancing back at the hearts and flowers, Jessica found herself thinking of Blake. Although she had made a decision to suppress all thoughts of a relationship, she couldn't help feeling a twinge of sadness as the "what-might-have-been" question came into her mind. *Stop it!* she ordered herself, screwing the letter into a ball and stuffing it in her pocket. *What's over is over and what never was will never be!*

"Good news, everyone," beamed Karen as she popped her head through the door. "The ratings are up!"

Belinda hurriedly concluded her call as Karen handed out several sheets of paper listing the ratings figures around the country for the night before. They were surprisingly good. In the new seven pm timeslot, *Bondi Place* was finishing a firm second behind Channel Thirteen's *Mystery Clue* in all major cities except for Melbourne.

"We have lots of publicity plans for Melbourne," Karen explained. "In fact, we're hoping to send some cast members down there very soon for special appearances. We'll let you know."

Karen collected the ratings sheets quickly and proceeded to head back out the door. She was just in time to collide with Holly. Relations between Holly and the network executives were still terse, despite the young starlet's attempts to apologise to everyone. Not a word was exchanged as the pair crossed paths.

All eyes were on Holly as she stood at the door. Sadie forced a half-hearted smile, Jared just stared and even Belinda didn't say a word. They were all seasoned performers and had a low opinion of youngsters who abused their positions. In their eyes, Holly was blatantly guilty of this.

"Hi, Holly," said Jessica, breaking the tension.

"You don't have to speak to me," Holly replied. "I know I'm off limits."

"Of course I will," said Jessica loudly. "Anyone who was a real friend would!"

Holly appreciated this support more than words could express. While she didn't blame the other cast members for turning their backs on her, she was still disappointed. Within seconds, Sadie, Jared and Belinda had left. The group of extras soon followed.

"I'm glad it's just the two of us," said Holly. "How are things with you and Blake? Have you managed to sort anything out?"

Jessica's face was a picture of heartbreak.

"Bad news?" Holly suggested.

Jessica allowed herself to weaken. "I thought it could happen, I truly did," she admitted. "I really liked him well, I guess I still do – but he doesn't feel the same way."

"That's not the impression I get," Holly pointed out. "He seems really happy about the publicity. I saw him collecting copies of *Remote Control* from around the canteen."

Jessica wasn't surprised. "That's just it – all he cares about is publicity. He doesn't like me at all. I'm just good for his career."

"Are you sure?" Holly asked.

"Afraid so," Jessica replied. "Claude told me his entire scheme."

"But then, how are you going to work alongside each other? You know Emily and Stefan are supposed to have a romance – you'll be in more scenes together than ever before."

Jessica wasn't looking forward to this. "I know. But I'm an actor – so I'll act. Act like everything is okay."

Holly was impressed by her friend's resolve. "Gosh

– I thought I had problems. I'd hate to be in your shoes."

Jessica sighed. *Don't I know it*, she thought.

* * *

The digital clock sitting beside the mattress that Blake had managed to squeeze into his cupboard-sized room read 10.05 am. The sun was up and a choir of birds were warming up their vocal chords outside the window. They had reached a glass-shattering crescendo before Blake was shocked into consciousness.

"Damn!" he yelled, realising he had overslept. "Dad!"

He jumped up and out of the makeshift bed and stumbled into the hall. Pushing his father's bedroom door open, he saw the older man, still fast asleep – probably hungover. Blake had asked his dad to wake him at seven am as his alarm wasn't working. But clearly it was far too much to expect.

He threw off his clothes and leapt into the shower, hoping that he could still make it to the studio on time.

He was due in make-up at ten-thirty, although it was likely that the preceding scenes were running overtime. This could buy him a little extra breathing space. What he didn't have time to do was to learn his lines – and this was something he could not cover.

After less than a minute in the shower, he stepped out and raced into the lounge room. Stark naked, he fumbled around in the boxes, still not unpacked, for clean clothes to wear. It was only then that he realised the birds had stopped singing, to be replaced by a muffled giggling sound. He looked out the window on to the ground floor balcony. A blind blocked most of the view, but a small gap below it usually allowed a stream of sunlight into the room. Something was blocking it. He walked over and pulled the cord, rocketing the blind upward in a split second. What he saw gave him the biggest shock of his life: seven teenage girls gathered at his window. For five full seconds he was paralysed, treating the fans to an unexpected exhibition of his naked body. Finally, he regained control of his senses and hastily pulled the blind down. *Oh my*

God! he thought to himself. *This is the most embarrassing moment of my life.*

By the time he had changed and raced out the door, his watch read fifteen minutes to eleven. As he stepped into the cab which would take him to Channel Eleven, he heard more giggling – the girls, who were all in school uniform, were still waiting outside his apartment block. *What am I going to do?* he wondered. *They know where I live! What if they decide to spy on me every day?*

However, of much more importance was the reception awaiting him at Channel Eleven. He had been late many times. Possibly one too many.

* * *

Lulu applied the final touches to Jessica's make-up. On this occasion, she was painted in a slightly different way. The Channel Eleven executives had ordered an "up market" look, which Lulu interpreted to mean thick black eyeliner and deep red lipstick. Regarding herself in the mirror, Jessica decided that she looked five years older. She wasn't sure if she liked it or not.

Gus appeared at the door. "We're ready for you, Jess," he said. "Where's Blake?"

This was a question Jessica and Lulu had been discussing. He was now almost half an hour late. Before they had a chance to report this to Gus, Blake burst through the door.

"I'm sorry I'm late," he said apologetically. "My alarm didn't go off."

While Gus and Lulu were unimpressed, Jessica found herself wondering if the real reason involved his father. She suspected Blake was having problems and making excuses to cover them up. If this was the case, her heart went out to him. She wanted to help, but couldn't bring herself to get close to him again. Not after everything that had happened.

Blake felt an overwhelming need to confide in Jessica. Even though they had only discussed his problems at home once, he had been greatly comforted and reassured by her support. He craved that feeling again. It was ironic that despite receiving a dozen fan letters a day and being well on his way to mediocre stardom, he had never felt more alone in his life. The fact that Jessica had offered him no reason for her change of heart made it all the more difficult.

"Hop in the chair and we'll make you up quickly," said Lulu, who had quite a soft spot for the young actor.

Blake had no choice but to follow her instruction as Gus and Jessica left to make their way to the studio.

Outside, Gus paused. "You go ahead," he said to Jessica. "I'll be with you in a minute. We can't start filming until Sleepyhead is ready anyway."

Jessica continued on towards the studio. Once she was out of earshot, Gus reached into his pocket and dialled a number on his mobile phone.

"Karen – it's Gus," he began. "He's just arrived. We can't put up with this for much longer. He's costing us time. And time is money."

At the other end of the line, Karen Wolfe was a very angry producer.

* * *

All eyes were on Blake as he made his way into the studio. Most of the crew were sitting around, bemoaning the likelihood of the delay adding extra time to their total working day.

Jessica used the time to polish her dialogue. The scene was set in the Surf Cafe and involved Emily and Stefan having an argument, ending with Stefan storming out to the beach. The scene to follow, when the episode finally went on air, was the one shot days earlier, where Stefan is bitten by the blue-ringed octopus and left for dead. It had taken Jessica all this time to get used to shooting scenes out of sequence, but she was now very adept at fast forwarding and rewinding her character's emotions as required. Blake, however, was not as fast a learner.

"I'm really sorry about all this," he said to Jessica as he took his mark on the set.

Thinking of his father, Jessica couldn't lose her temper. "Have you learned your lines?" she asked.

Blake shook his head. "Not all of them."

Michael, the director, appeared from his usual position in the control room. He was in a bad mood because of the delay and was not about to tolerate any further unprofessional behaviour from Blake.

"We have five minutes to do this scene," he said. "That's three takes at the most. Do you understand me?"

Blake nodded, but knew he was in big trouble.

By this time the crew had all assumed their regular positions. Blake and Jessica stood together, whispering so that their voices could not be recorded on the audio monitor taping the scene.

"What can I do?" asked Blake desperately.

Jessica knew she had two options. Either she performed her lines as she'd memorised them, which would make her look good and Blake appear extremely disorganised. Or, she could adapt her dialogue to suit whatever Blake could recall – so as to smooth over the parts he'd forgotten. Although this would alter the exact content of the scene, as long as the main idea was preserved Michael would probably accept it. Neither she nor Blake would come off well in this scenario, but at least the scene could be completed satisfactorily. After a moment of deliberation, she decided to sacrifice her hard work.

"I'll follow your lead," she assured Blake. "All you have to do is ask me how I feel about you. I tell you I'm not sure and you become upset and storm off in a huff."

The irony of this was not lost on either of them. The story-line could have been a page out of their own lives, but at this point in time, there was no opportunity to dwell on it.

"And action," shouted Gus.

Blake and Jessica launched into the scene. To Blake's surprise, he remembered the essence of his lines and improvised quite well. Jessica altered her performance to suit his and by the third take Michael was content.

Blake was overwhelmed with relief. "Thanks," he said to Jessica.

Jessica dropped her guard a little. "Yeah . . . well . . . we didn't have much choice."

Blake decided that this was a perfect opportunity. "Are you ready to tell me what's eating you yet?" he asked.

While Jessica's attitude toward him had softened, she was not keen to pursue the subject. "I think you know," she said simply.

* * *

Blake waited nervously in Karen Wolfe's office. He had a fair idea of why he had been summoned. *She wants to tell me off*, he figured. *I've really landed myself in it this time.*

Karen joined him. Her appearance seemed to disintegrate more and more with each passing day. Her once manicured hair and make-up were gone, her face hidden under the shadow of a *Bondi Place* baseball cap. Her expensive wardrobe had been discarded in favour of baggy tracksuit pants and a T-shirt. If Blake had not met her before, he would have assumed that she was one of the many cleaners who circulated the studio. Stress was not treating her kindly.

"I assume you have an idea why I've asked you here," Karen began.

Blake nodded, ashamed. "I know. I was late again. I'll make a better effort in future."

"Fair enough," Karen replied.

Blake was stunned. *Fair enough?* he repeated to himself. *That's all she's going to say?*

Karen reclined in her chair. "The main reason I wanted to see you is to talk about an important story-line we have coming up," she explained. "I was wary about just launching into it, because it will be very demanding for you. I need to know if you're up to it."

Blake wasn't sure what she was getting at. "You'll have to give me some more information," he said.

"You remember Terry Carmichael, the old Channel Eleven variety star you met at the shopping centre a couple of weeks ago?"

Blake smiled. "How could I forget?"

"From what I've heard, you two worked very well together that day. As a result, we're discussing the possibility of bringing him into the show to play your father."

Blake couldn't see any problem with this. "Sounds great," he replied.

Karen was pleased with his response. "Good. The reason I'm making a big deal of this is we want to do a major story-line with the two of you. One which will require a lot of effort and dedication on your behalf. It will put you at the forefront of the show, alongside your story with Jessica, of course."

"Of course," said Blake confidently, concealing his reservations about how the on-screen romance would actually progress.

Blake could see that Karen still had major concerns about giving him this heavy workload. Although he couldn't see any solution to his ongoing problems with his real father, he knew that he couldn't allow it to continue jeopardising his future. *This is a great opportunity*, he decided. *I have to assure Karen I'm up to it*.

"Count me in," he said. "I promise – no more mucking about from now on."

Karen wasn't totally convinced, but realised she would have to take the risk. "Okay – I'll tell the writers to go ahead."

Blake stood to leave, but realised there was an

important question he hadn't asked. "What is this big story-line anyway?"

Karen smiled. She was not aware of Blake's situation with his father so thought nothing of her reply. "Terry will be playing an alcoholic. The story will be about Stefan setting him on the straight and narrow."

Karen looked down at the papers on her desk, and didn't see Blake's stunned reaction. *How am I going to deal with this?* he asked himself. *How am I going to act out my own life on screen?*

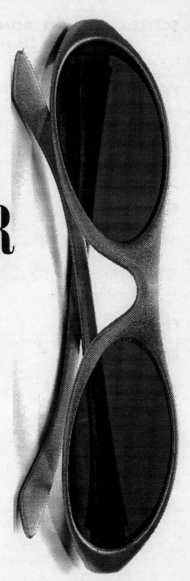

CHAPTER
SIX

SCENE 7. **INT. BONDI** **MORNING 4**
BEACH HOSPITAL

EMILY, STEFAN

STEFAN IS STILL IN A COMA, HIS BODY HOOKED UP WITH
WIRES TO NUMEROUS ITEMS OF MEDICAL EQUIPMENT.
EMILY MAINTAINS A PASSIONATE VIGIL BY HIS BEDSIDE.

EMILY
Please wake up, Stefan. There are so many things we haven't
done, so many things we haven't said to each other.

*STEFAN STIRS, EVER SO SLIGHTLY. EMILY IS TOO EMO-
TIONAL TO NOTICE.*

EMILY
I have never told you this before – but I love you. I want us to be
together – forever.

*STEFAN MOVES AGAIN, THIS TIME WITH MORE ENERGY.
EMILY PICKS UP ON IT.*

EMILY
Stefan – can you hear me? Stefan!

STEFAN'S EYES SPRING OPEN. EMILY IS ELATED.

EMILY
Thank God! Can you speak?

STEFAN
(GROGGILY) I love you, too. I want you to marry me.

EMILY
(shocked)
What?

STEFAN

I said, I want you to marry me.

OUT ON EMILY, THRILLED BY STEFAN'S APPARENT RECOVERY AND SHOCKED BY HIS UNEXPECTED PROPOSAL.

Studio Four had been transformed into Bondi Beach Hospital, with an ambulance parked outside and doctors and nurses milling about. Jessica's first impression was *My God! Sadie's finally had a heart attack!*

A logical explanation awaited. The ambulance was there to service a very dodgy-looking hospital set, which had been hastily pasted together by carpenters overnight. The doctors and nurses were all extras and the scene to be filmed involved Emily rushing Stefan to hospital after discovering him unconscious on the beach. Jessica was thrown – this wasn't what she was expecting.

"Michael," she said, attracting the director's attention. "What's going on? I thought we were doing these scenes tomorrow at a real hospital."

Michael took Jessica aside. "You haven't heard?" he asked quietly.

Jessica was thrown. "Heard what?"

"Geraldo's been sacked. Happened last night. All the scripts are being re-written. We've had to bring these scenes forward and into the studio."

Jessica was shocked by this news. *Geraldo sacked?*

She knew better than to probe Michael for details – as director, he was bound to know the full story and equally bound to secrecy. *Far better to ask the tea lady*, she decided.

The reason for the shuffle in scenes and locations was still a mystery. Jessica had learned not to question such occurrences – the explanation was, no doubt, long and complicated. Of more importance was the fact that she had not yet memorised her lines for this new scene.

"Hi, Jessica," said a Blake-like voice from behind her.

Jessica turned around to discover that it was, indeed, the bearer of her confused feelings of both affection and contempt. "Hi," she said awkwardly. "Have you heard about all this?"

Blake nodded. "Yep. We have to do some very fast rehearsing. For once I'm ahead of you. I got these new scenes half an hour ago. Do you want to rehearse together?"

Although Jessica didn't want to be around Blake for any longer than was strictly necessary, she realised that she had little choice – the rescheduled scenes had to be memorised. It made sense for them to step aside and concentrate in peace.

"Let's find a quiet spot and sit down," she replied.

They walked in silence for a couple of minutes before settling on a piece of pavement just outside the studio, close enough for them to see what was going on, but distant enough to provide some solitude.

Jessica flipped through the pages of the new script, which included several unexpected scenes inserted to replace the ones Geraldo was to have been in. Meanwhile, Blake searched her face for signs of recognition of their personal situation. When they were on set together the other day, he'd had the feeling that Jessica was warming to him again. *Why else would she save me from humiliation?* he decided. *If I'm ever going to find out what the problem is, I have to keep pushing.*

Jessica could feel he was watching her and maintained a facade of professional indifference. She had thought about it in bed the night before, and decided to pretend that she and Blake had never kissed and had no personal history at all.

Blake couldn't stand it any longer. "When are you going to talk to me?" he demanded.

Jessica glanced up from the script. "We're here to do a job. Let's do it," she said impassively. Deep down, it was hurting her to even look him in the eye.

Blake, however, was not about to take no for an answer. He ripped the script from her hands. "Talk to me, Jessica!" he insisted. "What's going on? One minute I think we're on together, the next minute you're treating me like I'm the invisible man!"

Jessica was stunned. She matched his temper, her brown eyes piercing his blue. "You used me. You lied to me and you used me."

Blake was genuinely confused. "What are you talking about?" he asked.

Jessica considered explaining, but dismissed the idea. She believed that he knew exactly what she was talking about and was simply playing dumb. And recalling the details for his benefit was far too painful. She grabbed her copy of the script from him and rose to her feet.

"Learn the scene on your own," she said. "Make

sure you know it word for word. If you don't – I won't
be saving you this time."

Jessica turned on her heel and strode back to the
production office. Blake was knocked for six. He
stood up and called after her.

"Jessica!"

But she kept on walking.

Blake slumped back down onto the pavement. *I give
up*, he decided. *I don't know what her problem is – but
it's not going to be mine any longer. We're through!*

Only then did he look at his copy of the revised
script. The first three scenes required almost no effort
on his behalf at all – Stefan was to remain unconscious
in a hospital bed, while the other characters talked at
his bedside. The fourth scene was a different story.
Blake didn't know whether to laugh or cry as the
words sunk in – Stefan proposes marriage to Emily!
How on earth are we going to do this? he asked himself.
*We can't be nice to each other for five minutes – how are
we going to pretend to be hopelessly in love?*

* * *

Jessica was relieved to find the Green Room empty, providing her with the perfect environment to memorise the rescheduled scenes. She sat down and began to flick through the pages. She was overwhelmed by the amount of dialogue allocated to Emily in the first three scenes – and positively shocked by the content of the fourth. *Marriage!* The idea ricocheted back and forward through her head – not only the ceremony, but dozens of intense one-on-one scenes with Blake which would lead to this development. *No way!* Her hands trembled as she read the gushing dialogue.

Soon Holly invaded her peace and quiet, plonking herself and several textbooks on the sofa. "That's it!" she declared. "No more sessions with mad, bad Hettie for me!"

Holly was referring to Hettie MacDonald, the *Bondi Place* tutor with whom she and Jessica had been studying since the show began production. While Jessica looked forward to the sessions, Holly attended under protest.

"Now that I've been sacked I'm not going back," she said, waving an assignment with the grade "D –"

scrawled on one corner in red ink. "That woman doesn't know a good essay from the cheap perfume she wears! I don't care that I've still got two weeks on the show – I'm finished with her!"

Jessica felt compelled to point out some harsh realities. "I hate to be the one to tell you this," she began, "but your dad is going to make you go back to school once this is all over. If Hettie flunks you, you'll have to go back and start Year Eleven from scratch."

The thought terrified Holly. "Forget it! I'm not dropping back a year with those losers at Ballina High. Besides, Darren says I'm going to be flat out attending auditions."

Jessica looked encouragingly at her friend, which had the opposite effect – Holly realised that she was fooling herself.

"Okay, so maybe I won't be *that* busy with auditions," she admitted.

Jessica was unconvinced. Holly knew exactly what she was implying.

"But I can't go back a year," she insisted. "If only there was something I could do to save my job."

Holly flung the text books on the floor, in an expression of desperate and pathetic rage. It was then that she noticed the corner of an envelope on the floor beneath the couch. She reached down and picked it up. Opening it, she skimmed ahead to read the final line on the scented paper. It was the fan letter Jessica had received from Ralph.

"Hopelessly devoted to you," Holly read. "Who *is* this whacko?"

Jessica smiled. "I don't know – but at least somebody is devoted to me," she replied, thinking of Blake.

"Do you mind if I read it?" Holly asked, already reading on.

"Go ahead," Jessica assured her all the same. "Claude has read it anyway. He's screening all our mail."

Holly read the letter, pausing only to emit sounds which suggested both envy and amusement. Holly had never received such a passionate letter. Although Ralph was probably the biggest loser on the planet, it was still flattering that he bothered to write.

"I wish I got mail like this," she moaned.

Jessica looked up from the script. "Maybe you do," she replied. "Apparently, the reason Claude reads all the mail first is to stop any offensive or disturbing letters reaching us. You may have lots of fans out there you don't even know about."

Holly considered this. She looked over to Blake's pigeon hole which was overflowing with letters. "He's popular," she mused.

Jessica looked over at the collection of letters. "Mmm," she said. "I'd say his position around here is pretty safe."

Holly walked over to the cappuccino machine, passing the pigeon holes on her way. All of a sudden an idea occurred to Jessica.

"I've got it!" she said.

"What are you talking about?" Holly asked.

Jessica paused for a moment to allow her words to have maximum impact – a trick she had learned on the show. "I think I know how to save your job."

*		*		*

The front door swung open and Agnes Harrison smiled warmly. "Welcome to our home," she said. "It's lovely to see you again."

Jessica stepped inside. Moments like these baffled her – Aunt Agnes seemed like a kind and loving woman, yet Holly slagged her off at every opportunity. Before Jessica had a chance to step into the living room, Holly appeared from her bedroom which veered off halfway down the hall.

"Hi. Have you brought all the stuff?" she asked excitedly.

Jessica waved the bag in her hand. "Your future is in here," she assured her.

"What are you talking about?" asked Aunt Agnes.

Holly smiled. "Let's just say I may not be going back to Ballina as soon as expected," she explained. "I hope you won't mind having me around a little longer."

Aunt Agnes was confused. "Since when do you ever ask me what I think!" she retorted, in a tone which assured them she was only half serious. "I'll leave you to it."

The older woman disappeared to the kitchen, promising home-made cake and biscuits in a few minutes' time. Holly led Jessica into the living room. It was only then that she realised it was the first time her co-star had visited her at home.

"It's nothing much," Holly admitted of the surroundings. "Nothing like your mansion."

Jessica, however, didn't care where Holly lived. "It's very sweet," she said. "And I think you're being too hard on your aunt. She's not that bad!"

"Yeah, yeah, yeah," Holly replied – she'd heard this a thousand times before. "Now let's get started."

Jessica tipped the contents of her bag on the floor. It contained paper, pens and hundreds of envelopes in different sizes and colours. Boxes of chocolates also spilled out, followed by some cheap perfume. The last item to emerge was the most baffling of all.

"What on earth are these for?" Holly asked, holding up a pair of Calvin Klein men's underpants.

"Just an extra touch," Jessica replied with a smile. "I actually bought them for my dad last Christmas, but he never wears them."

Holly laughed. The girls proceeded to get down to the task at hand – filling every envelope with a fan letter addressed to Holly. The chocolates, perfume and underwear were intended as gifts from male admirers.

"This plan is foolproof," Jessica assured her. "Claude keeps a running total of all the letters we get, which goes straight to Karen. Once these letters come in and she realises how popular you are, there's no way they can write Racine out of the show."

"I hope you're right," said Holly. "I'd hate to get my hopes up and then have it all fall through."

"Trust me," said Jessica.

She took the lid off a pen and began to scrawl a letter. 'DEAR HOLLY – I THINK YOU ARE HOT. RACINE IS MY FAVOURITE CHARACTER ON THE SHOW. I WANT TO FATHER YOUR CHILDREN.'

Holly laughed as she read Jessica's ramblings. She attempted a version of her own. It read: 'DEAR HOLLY. I THINK YOU HAVE A BETTER BODY THAN ELLE MACPHERSON, ARE A BETTER

ACTRESS THAN NICOLE KIDMAN AND
SHOULD RECORD A POP SINGLE.'

"Do you think I'm overdoing it?" she asked Jessica.

Jessica shook her head. "The more compliments,
the better. Might be a good idea to stuff the Calvin
Kleins in with that one."

Holly signed an illegible name and stuffed the letter
and the underwear in an envelope. Only then did
something else occur to her.

"Who is going to pay the postage on all this?"

Jessica regarded her with a sheepish smile. "You
have to spend money to make money," she reminded
her. "I come up with the idea – you provide the cash!"

Holly decided this was a pretty fair deal. *After all,
how much could it cost? Not that much, surely.*

Three hours later they had sealed almost four
hundred envelopes. Holly quickly revised her assess-
ment. *That's a lot of money!* she realised. Then she
thought of Jessica's advice. *But it will be worth it in the
end!*

* * *

Blake tossed and turned in his bed, fighting the demon of a deep and restless sleep. His mind was like a fast-moving kaleidoscope, image after image blurring into each other. Some pictures seemed to involve a wedding, the others a funeral. He could see a bride walking down the aisle, passing a crowd of onlookers – some dressed in black, others in white. He recognised Sadie, Belinda and Jared sitting in the front pew. The bride stopped at the end. Then, in another sequence, punctuated by blinding strikes of light and darkness, the bride lifted her veil. Underneath, Jessica's face smiled. Seconds later, it disintegrated into a bitter frown. The camera in his mind travelled to where the groom would traditionally stand. In its place, a coffin. Finally, amid another chaotic clash of colours, the coffin lid eased open. Blake saw himself lying still, his arms folded across his chest. Dead. He awakened with a jolt.

Sitting up, he turned on the light. His body was glistening with perspiration, his heart beating a million miles an hour. *What happened?* he asked himself, observing his sheets were damp with sweat. His nightmare returned in sharp grabs – his fellow cast members in the audience, Jessica a bride . . . and his own body in the coffin. *It must have something to do with Stefan and Emily's wedding*, he decided. *Everyone from the show was there . . .*

He got up and stumbled into the kitchen, following a trail of light into the living room. His father was sitting at the table, a three-quarters empty bottle of Scotch whisky in front of him. Blake stood in the doorway for a moment. The sight of Eddie was heartbreaking – a man with many years ahead of him, looking much older than he should. The thought of his upcoming *Bondi Place* story-line with Terry Carmichael was alarming. It was going to be very painful to act out the scenario he experienced daily at home.

Blake joined him at the table. Father and son stared at each other in an unspoken acknowledgment of the situation. Eddie's eyes expressed remorse, Blake's condemnation. He wanted to talk to his father about the dream, but Eddie was in no position to listen – let alone offer any words of reassurance.

Finally, Blake spoke. "This has got to stop. We have

a new home – this is supposed to be a fresh start."

Eddie's mouth opened slowly to express the only words his inebriated brain could formulate. "I'm sorry," he moaned. "I've got problems."

Blake reached over and grabbed Eddie's empty glass and the bottle of whisky. The older man looked at him, desperation clouding his face. "Please, don't," he muttered, fearing Blake would do as he'd done many times before – and tip the bottle down the sink.

However, Blake removed the cap and poured a full glass of the translucent, chestnut-coloured substance. He raised the glass to his mouth and consumed the fiery liquid in three gulps. His throat burned from the sensation. As the alcohol made its way into his bloodstream, the room rotated in slow, semi-circular motions. Sitting opposite, Eddie's disapproving but helpless face seemed to magnify with every turn. Eddie may have been drunk but he could see what his son was doing. His greatest fear was that Blake would turn out like him.

Blake slammed the glass down on the table. "I've got problems too," he said.

The two men sat face to face for half an hour, neither breaking the eye contact. Eddie didn't reach for the bottle throughout, giving Blake one minor victory.

Finally, Eddie nodded off.

Blake returned to his bedroom, where once again, images from his nightmare haunted him, intensifying as the alcohol invaded his system. He concluded that it was a premonition indicating that any relationship with Jessica was doomed, but more frightening than this, that something tragic might be just around the corner.

He lay down and stared at the ceiling. The room was filled with uncomfortable vibes. He would not sleep there that night.

He rose a second time and wandered back out to the kitchen. He stumbled toward his father's bedroom, ignoring the sight and sound of Eddie snoozing in the living room.

He walked into the master bedroom and sat on Eddie's bed. The floor was littered with everything imaginable. One item attracted Blake's particular

interest. He picked up the scrapbook and was amazed
to find it filled with press clippings charting his own
stardom. Even the smallest mentions had been
proudly cut out of the paper and displayed. Blake
knew the owner of the scrapbook could be no-one but
his father.

He lay down on his father's bed, hugging the book
to his chest. The anger and sadness of just a few
minutes ago was overwhelmed by affection. *Dad did
this for me*, he thought to himself.

He slept fitfully for the rest of the night, partly due
to the noise of his father snoring in the living room –
but mostly out of fear that his nightmare would return.
Each wail of Eddie's nasal breath reminded him of
another good memory from his childhood. Happy
times. *Times that will never be again*, he reminded
himself sadly.

The issue of how he would cope with acting out this
scenario on *Bondi Place* was also nagging at his mind.

CHAPTER
SEVEN

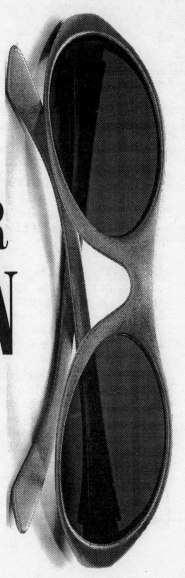

MEMO

TO: JESSICA FAIRGATE
           BLAKE DEXTER

FROM: CLAUDE DESUSA

RE: CHANNEL ELEVEN
           PUBLICITY, MELBOURNE

CC: KAREN WOLFE

This is to confirm the details of our trip to Melbourne this weekend for the annual charity telethon.

Stars from all Channel Eleven programmes, as well as pop stars, sports figures and politicians will be participating in the ten-hour broadcast. Apart from the number one aim which is to raise money for charity, this is an excellent opportunity to talk about the show.

I will be flying to Melbourne on Thursday night; however, according to the filming schedule, you will both be required on set. Bookings have been made for you to follow me down on Friday morning. I will meet you at the Melbourne studios and brief you on the run-down of the event.

Claude

Claude DeSusa's desk was a mess. Magazines, paper and letters were stacked on top of each other in a disorderly manner. It was truly amazing that the publicist managed to do any work amid this chaos.

Jessica and Blake sat opposite Claude as he talked animatedly on the phone. Blake had hardly slept the night before and was extremely tired. He also felt awkward around Jessica. She, however, was totally preoccupied with searching Claude's desk with her eyes for the fan letters she and Holly had sent in. As Claude continued to speak on the phone, she watched him open a familiar-looking parcel. He retrieved a letter and the Calvin Klein underwear and smiled.

"Goodbye, then," said Claude into the phone. He looked at the size of the underwear. "Perfect. I'll be able to fit into these!"

Jessica was amazed. *So that's what happens to most of the presents people send us!* she thought. Nonetheless, she was happy to see Claude mark the letter in his book. She was sure the information would be passed on to Karen and work in Holly's favour.

"I've got exciting news," Claude announced, snapping back to the subject in hand. "You two are off to Melbourne this weekend."

Jessica and Blake were less than enthused. *Melbourne? Together?*

"The annual Channel Eleven telethon," he continued. "It's to raise money for kids in hospital. Seeing you are our star couple, I can't think of two better people to send."

Blake and Jessica grimaced. *If ever there is a time to put a stop to this, it's now*, Jessica thought. Blake, however, had a different approach. *If Jessica's not going to tell me what's going on, why not exploit this as much as we can? Maybe then she'll be forced to come out with the truth.*

"Sounds great," said Blake. "We'll make everyone think we're the hottest item since Romeo and Juliet."

Jessica was horrified. Blake had just confirmed her theory. *He's not even trying to make a secret of it! He's using me and doesn't care if I know it or not!*

Claude was thrilled. "Wonderful!" he beamed. Noticing Jessica still had reservations, he reached over the desk and took her hand. "Think of the kids the money raised could help. Once the suckers out in Viewer Land see an attractive couple like you begging for donations, the cash registers are bound to ring."

Jessica didn't follow this logic at all. Aware that his argument made no sense, Claude rose quickly from his chair before she had time to argue.

"I've got a meeting with the morning paper," he said as he grabbed his jacket. "I'll send you a memo with all the details. It should be a great weekend."

Claude beat a hasty retreat. Jessica looked angrily at Blake. He responded to her stare with a raised eyebrow. There was nothing either could say.

* * *

Charles Kingsford Smith Airport is not among the best airports of the world. Though its close proximity to the city makes access easy, the distance between its domestic and international terminals can be confusing to disorientated foreigners. On this busy Friday morning, a group of Japanese tourists were having a particularly stressful time working out where they should be.

"Can-I-help-you?" Blake asked slowly, noting their distress.

The oldest woman in the group offered her ticket.

"You have to catch a bus to the international terminal," Blake explained. "Then you can board your plane for Tokyo."

The oldest man pointed to his hand luggage. It took a few minutes for Blake to comprehend his concern. Taking another look at the ticket, he realised that the group had just stepped off a domestic flight from Perth and were worried about their luggage.

"Don't worry," he assured them. "You've only got one ticket so all of your bags will be forwarded."

He pointed them in the direction of the connecting airport bus and waved them away with a smile.

Jessica watched the exchange with a mixture of sadness and affection. She truly believed Blake was a caring person and this act of kindness seemed to prove it. But it only made the failure of their budding relationship even more poignant.

They made their way to the departure lounge, exchanging only forced pleasantries, to discover that their flight to Melbourne was running a full hour later than scheduled. The wait proved uncomfortable, not only because of their own strained conversation but because all eyes were upon them.

After staring at them for some time, a young girl approached Jessica. "Are you Emily from *Bondi Place*?" she asked.

Jessica confirmed it with a nod and a smile. She expected to be asked to sign an autograph for the girl, but she scurried off. Jessica watched her whisper something in her mother's ear. Within a minute, mother and five children, ranging from a baby to a teenager, were practically sitting on Blake and Jessica's laps.

"What's it like being on the show?" the woman asked excitedly. "I read in *Remote Control* that you two are a couple. You look very cute together."

Jessica looked accusingly at Blake. He read her mind. She was thinking, *This is all your fault!*

An overhead announcement indicated that the flight

was ready for boarding. Jessica and Blake politely extricated themselves from their admirers and joined the queue to present their tickets.

Blake looked over Jessica's shoulder and caught a glimpse of her seat allocation. "We're not sitting together?" he observed with surprise.

"That's right," Jessica replied quietly, so that their adoring public wouldn't hear. "I asked to be put as far away from you as possible."

Blake realised the day was going to be a very bumpy ride.

* * *

Storm clouds circled the sky, threatening to dump unseasonal rain on the Victorian capital of Melbourne. But the city which gave birth to Australian Rules Football and Kylie Minogue was well known for its four-seasons-in-a day climate. Anything could happen.

Blake and Jessica had been travelling in the taxi from the airport for a full twenty minutes, both stubbornly refusing to offer a word of conversation. Despite their pretence at disinterest, it was evident that their minds were full of thoughts of each other. They were also aware that when they appeared on Channel Eleven Melbourne's annual charity telethon, the studio audience would be expecting a happy couple. The reality couldn't be more different.

The taxi turned into a street. "This is it," said the driver. "The closest thing Melbourne has to Hollywood!"

Jessica looked toward Blake coldly. "Don't make this any more difficult than it has to be," she warned.

Blake was beginning to regret he'd ever gone along with Claude's scheme. His hope that this experience would bring them closer together had gone disastrously wrong.

* * *

Channel Eleven Melbourne was often regarded as a poor relation to its Sydney affiliate, with the stations competing to produce the highest quality and most popular shows. The result, however, was usually a compromise. They refused to co-operate with each other and this affected their ability to produce anything successful. Over the last few years, most executive decisions had been made in Sydney which led employees at the Melbourne station to feel like part of a malnourished underdog. As *Bondi Place* was a Sydney production, there was a reluctance in the southern capital to make it a success. Not surprisingly, the ratings figures in Melbourne were not good.

Studio Eight was located at the back corner of the bustling Channel Eleven complex, providing little competition for the towering city skyline. Its stark grey-brick construction contrasted with the muddy Yarra River which flowed lazily along its other side.

Claude accompanied Jessica and Blake from the administration building to the studio entrance. He was typically nervous about the day ahead.

"Whatever you do – remember to smile," he insisted. "This telethon is great exposure for the show. Plug it at every opportunity." He paused, considering how to broach another subject without sounding too crass and insensitive. "And if anybody asks you about a real-life relationship, remember, you are a hot item. That's guaranteed to get us in tomorrow morning's gossip columns."

Blake and Jessica realised it was pointless to argue. They had no option but to play the loving couple. The first test came when a bus pulled up beside the studio and a crowd of the enthusiastic audience jumped out.

"Blake! Jessica!" cried one particularly excited teenager.

"Hold hands," Claude muttered.

Blake took Jessica's hand in his. Her grip was warm and soft and Blake couldn't help enjoying the brief sensation. However, the second they stepped into the backstage area of the studio the act was over. Their hands parted, but not without a mutual realisation – the attraction was still very much alive.

Claude led them toward the set, where the crew were setting up in preparation for the beginning of the telethon. A long panel had been constructed with the donation telephone number displayed at the front, illuminated by tacky neon lights. Each panel member had a plaque with their name on it. Jessica and Blake were seated at the far end, together. Beside Jessica was tennis ace Eugene Kennedy, a young gun from Darwin who had attracted a lot of publicity recently owing to his extraordinary ascent into the nation's top ranking. Blake was placed beside gold medal swimmer Kathy Bostock, who had been in the news of late but for a very different reason – she was suspected of deliberately colliding with a competitor at a recent trial. The verdict was still out and her presence at this event was bound to cause controversy.

Blake and Jessica took their seats. Keen to avoid talking to each other, they turned to their celebrity co-stars and attempted to have a conversation. "So what do you do, Eugene?" Jessica asked.

"I'm ranked number four in Australia," he replied, in a confident but not cocky manner.

Jessica was embarrassed that she didn't know this. She used to love keeping up with current affairs and sport, but this had become impossible since *Bondi Place*. It was a thrill to be sitting next to someone so talented.

Meanwhile, Blake was having a little more luck with Kathy. He was aware of her infamy and decided to get on her good side. "I think it's terrible the way the press have crucified you," he assured her.

Kathy, however, was completely unfazed. "I think it's great," she replied. "I don't care what anyone says – a little bit of controversy is good for the profile, which is good for sponsorship. And that means my bank balance."

Blake identified with this idea to some extent. "I agree. What good is being famous if you can't use it to your advantage?"

Jessica overheard his comment. If she had needed further confirmation of Blake's motives in forming a public alliance with her, this was it. She turned back to Eugene, regarding him with warm and fascinated eyes.

"Tell me more about yourself," she asked, loud enough for Blake to hear.

Throughout the banter which followed they stole regular glances at each other. Although they would not have admitted it, the emotion being exhibited was jealousy. The sight of the other enjoying talking to a member of the opposite sex – especially specimens so attractive and successful – was difficult to bear.

"We're on in ten," shouted Ronny Miller, the compere of the event. He was an instantly recognisable personality and only worked once a year on programs such as this. "Everybody look happy!"

* * *

Holly raced eagerly into the Green Room to check her pigeon hole. Just as she and Jessica had planned, it was overflowing with fan mail which she knew would have been registered already by Claude. *This will surely reverse management's decision to sack me!* she enthused.

She sat down on the couch to rehearse her lines, confident her future was looking bright. As she read through her dialogue, she became aware of the presence of someone else in the room. She looked up to see a figure standing at the door.

"Hi," said Holly. "Are you lost? Do you need some help?"

"No," was the reply. "Actually, this is kind of awkward but I suppose we should get it over and done with. I start on the show next week."

Holly smiled. "That's great. What part will you be playing?"

A pause, then an answer. "This is going to come as quite a shock to you – I'm playing your role. I'm taking over the part of Racine."

Holly was gobsmacked. "What? You can't be serious?"

"I'm afraid I am. I've just signed the contract. When Karen said she wasn't planning to tell you until next week . . . well, I thought it was only fair I break the news. I'd hate there to be any unpleasantness between us."

Holly was totally floored.

"I'm sorry," the girl repeated.

No answer from Holly.

Samantha Murdoch turned and left the room, very pleased with herself.

* * *

One hour into the telethon and Jessica and Blake were looking anything but loving. The donations were pouring in quickly and it was time for the celebrities to read some of them out.

Jessica was nervous when it came to her turn. She regarded the tiny slip of paper which had just been handed to her. "I've got one from Ralph of Sydney. He says he'll donate one hundred dollars and double it if I say I'm hopelessly devoted to him on air." She looked at the camera and smiled, happy to fulfil his wish for the sake of the donation. "So, Ralph, I'm hopelessly devoted to you. That's two hundred dollars you owe us."

The camera moved along to Blake. Only then did Jessica make the connection. *This guy Ralph – he's the fan who wrote me that letter.*

* * *

Sydney Harbour was calm. The grey-blue sky was reflected in the water, giving it an extra dimension with the contrast of shade and sunshine. The scene was observed from a window in Jessica's bedroom.

Heavy footsteps moved from the window to her bed. The figure of a man cast a large shadow over the sheets. A pile of clean washing lay on top of them, waiting to be put away. A strong, weathered hand extended forward and picked up a lacy bra. The man lifted it to his face, enjoying its softness and smell.

He walked over to the dressing table and picked up a hair brush. He ran it through his shoulder-length blonde hair with long, sensual strokes. He noticed an envelope resting beside an antique jewellery box. He picked it up, his face registering delight. The hearts and flowers pasted on the envelope were still intact.

"You got my letter," said Ralph. "Now I'm going to get you."

CHAPTER EIGHT

Win a date with a star of

BONDI PLACE

Yes, *TV Glamour Girls* is giving you the opportunity to wine and dine with the beautiful mega-babe Jessica Fairgate, who plays spunky Emily on the sun-drenched show *Bondi Place*. You will be picked up in a limousine and eat at one of Sydney's funkiest restaurants – The Bondi Sand Castle – which also happens to be located on the real life street where they film the hit show!

All you have to do is write in and tell us why – in twenty-five words or less – the fiery flame-haired Jessica is your ideal chick. The only other condition is keep it clean!

Good luck, everyone!

The early morning sun shone over Bondi Beach, casting golden light on the smooth sand and making the waves sparkle with reflections. Jessica and Holly emerged from the make-up van parked on Campbell Parade, the glamorous stretch of cappuccino culture which was awakening to the promise of a glorious new day.

"I can't believe they've hired somebody else to play my role," said Holly, the aftermath of tears still glistening in her eyes. "After everything we've done – all those letters – now it seems like it was all for nothing."

Jessica wished she could offer more words of consolation. "We gave it our best shot," she said. "Believe me – I don't like the thought of working with that cow Samantha Murdoch. I bet she slept with someone to get the part."

Holly forced a half-hearted chuckle. She appreciated that Jessica was trying to cheer her up. Only then did she realise she hadn't asked Jessica how things were going for her. "How was Melbourne?" she said.

Jessica shrugged. "Nice city. I've never been there

before. The shopping is just mad – but I didn't have time for much of that."

Holly looked knowingly at her friend. "You know what I mean. How were things with Blake?"

"Oh, I know he still wants us to pretend to be a couple. What he wants in real life, well . . ." She paused. "I'm beginning to sound like a broken record. I just don't know what to believe."

Holly was sympathetic. "Look, I've only got one week left on this show. There's not much I can say or do to help you, except to offer my own little observation. And that is, he likes you. But he's scared. He's scared to commit to you – he's scared you won't like him back."

Jessica looked out at the ocean. The sea breeze was seductive, just like Blake. But if she looked hard enough she could also see a storm cloud in the distance – and that was sobering. That was reality.

"I don't want to talk about it," she said. "Some things are just not meant to be."

They continued to walk down to the water's edge, where the film crew were setting up for the next scene.

Stripping off their dressing gowns to reveal a matching pair of bikinis, they became aware of a crowd of people watching. This was not unusual – people were intrigued by the cameras and, since the show had picked up in the ratings, fans were beginning to hound the cast and crew. All seemingly harmless – except for the figure watching the scene through binoculars, sitting undetected in the obscurity of a beaten up old utility building. Ralph kept the viewfinder fastened on Jessica, his eyes dancing over her every move. His excitement was increasing by the second, and his obsession growing dangerous.

* * *

The door to Claude DeSusa's office was closed. Inside, the publicist and producer of *Bondi Place* were having an intense discussion.

"Look at all these letters," said Claude, indicating the stack of mail piled on a chair.

"I'm not surprised," said Karen. "Blake's a very popular boy."

Claude picked up one of the parcels and held the name of the addressee toward Karen. "But they're not for Blake. They're for Holly. Everybody loves her — and we've just sacked her!"

Karen paused. "Really? All these letters for her? Why all of a sudden?"

Claude shrugged. "Maybe the public are on her side. Maybe they agree with all that stuff in *Remote Control*. Maybe they think we're the bad guys in all this."

Karen found it very hard to believe. In all her years as a producer she'd never encountered such an overwhelming response from the public. However, unlike some people in the television industry, she honestly respected feedback from the public. This development was to be taken very seriously.

"It's too late to keep her," she mused. "We've already signed Samantha Murdoch to take over the role."

Claude sighed. "I guess we'll just have to accept we've made a big mistake."

The look on Karen's face suggested otherwise.

"We'll see," she said. "Give me some time to think about it."

* * *

"Another character?" Holly repeated. "You want me to stay on the show – but play someone else?"

Karen realised the concept sounded ludicrous. However, she'd done her research and discovered some justification. "They've done it on American daytime soaps. I don't see why we can't do it here."

Holly needed time to absorb this news. "You really, really want me to stay?"

Karen nodded. "Of course – we'll have to give you a couple of weeks off. We'll change your hair, maybe send you to the solarium to improve your tan. A new image – and a whole new character. The publicity will be incredible."

Holly smiled and looked heavenward. *Someone has just saved my life*, she thought.

* * *

In the dead of night, the cool breeze floating off the tranquil water of Sydney harbour seemed conniving, laced with hidden motives. It approached the shore with calmness, but suddenly changed velocity, lashing trees and houses with a vengeance.

Jessica sat in her room on the first floor of her family home, listening to the wind rattle the shutters outside her window. She was busy learning her lines for the following morning, but had the disconcerting feeling of being watched. She stood up and walked to her window. Pulling back the curtains, she could see past the balcony and down to the garden below. There was not a soul in sight. *It must be my imagination*, she decided. *Maybe it's because Mum and Dad are out. I'm just being paranoid.*

Turning back to her room, she walked over to the bed. She sat down and looked over to her dressing table. Everything was as it always was, yet she felt an indefinable spookiness. The presence of somebody else.

Suddenly, the French doors leading to the balcony sprang open. Jessica turned around with a jolt. She heard the scurry of footsteps. Then a heavy thump, as if someone had just jumped to the ground below.

She raced out of her room and down the stairs. *I've got to call the police*, she decided. As she moved to the phone in the hall, she saw a figure outside the front door. She screamed in terror. The handle turned and the door burst open.

"What's going on?" said Blake, who had been about to knock. "Are you okay?"

Jessica was in shock. "It's you. I heard somebody on the balcony outside my room. It was you!"

Blake shook his head. He was alarmed by what Jessica was telling him. "No. I just got here."

Jessica calmed herself, but only a little.

"What's this about someone else? You say they were on your bedroom balcony?"

Jessica nodded. "I'm sure. It wasn't my imagination."

She would get no argument from Blake. He reached into his pocket and produced an envelope. He deliberated for a moment. Finally, he opened it.

"I don't think it's your imagination either," he said.

"I just received this letter. From some fruitcake named Ralph. It was sent to my house – he knows where I live."

The name sent a shiver up Jessica's spine. *Ralph – the guy who sent me the letter, the guy who rang during the telethon.*

She hesitated, frightened of what Blake might be about to say. After further deliberation, Blake realised he had to come out with it.

"He wrote that I have to break up with you," he began. "He said if I don't – he'll kill both of us."

Blake reached out and took Jessica in his arms. Her fear was like electricity, surging out of control.

"I'm scared," she admitted. "I'm really, really scared."

Blake looked into her eyes. "I know. But I'll protect you. I'll never let anyone hurt you." He hesitated, as if wondering whether to go that one step further. Finally, he realised he had nothing to lose. "I just want us to be together."

Jessica took comfort in his arms. "I want that too," she said.

They embraced passionately, unaware that they were being observed through the open door. Ralph was considering his next move.

**To find out more why
not read the rest of the Bondi
Place series – see the order
form at the back of this book!**

If you enjoyed this why not read the next book in the Bondi series:

BONDI PLACE
THE CRUELLEST CUT

Jason Herbison

Nominations are in and votes are being counted . . .
It's award time again and tempers are fraying . . .
Holly's got the hots for a top new talent
Jessica's courting trouble with an unknown admirere
And Blake saves a friend's back – but puts himself in
danger . . .

h Another Hodder Children's Book

BONDI PLACE
MONEY TALKS

Jason Herbison

Being a household name means money, money,
money – but there's always a price to pay . . .
Blake's in line for mega money but can he cope?
Jessica has a new rival – in love.
Holly has got herself in to trouble – again!

Another Hodder Children's Book

BONDI PLACE
THE BIG DECISION

Jason Herbison

Everyone knows that Blake and Jessica are an
item – on- and off-screen, but now Jessica has a
rival – someone who is determined to have Blake
all for herself. While Blake has to choose between
Jessica and his scheming co-star, Holly is made an
offer she can't refuse . . .

Another Hodder Children's Book

BONDI PLACE
CHART SENSATION

Jason Herbison

Jessica and Blake are back together and more in
love than ever, but there's always trouble in
paradise . . . Blake is in for a nasty surprise,
Jessica is caught up in a moral dilemma, and
Holly comes face to face with her past . . .

If you enjoyed this why not read:

MODELS
ZOË'S STORY

Chloë Rayban

With drama school fees mounting and few acting opportunities coming her way, Zoë jumps at the chance to earn extra money modelling. But as her modelling career takes off, Zoë finds it hard to hang on to her dream – and her man.

From commercials in Havana, auditions in Hollywood to super soap stardom, this is Zoë's story: a rollercoaster tale of friendship, romance, hard work and soaring success. But will she ever make it on to the stage?

BONDI PLACE

0 340 68335 X	3: The Cruellest Cut	£3.99	☐
0 340 73282 2	4: Money Talks	£3.99	☐
0 340 73283 0	5: The Big Decision	£3.99	☐
0 340 73284 9	6: Chart Sensation	£3.99	☐

All Hodder Children's books are available at your local bookshop or newsagent, or can be ordered direct from the publisher. Just tick the titles you want and fill in the form below. Prices and availability subject to change without notice.

Hodder Children's Books, Cash Sales Department, Bookpoint, 39 Milton Park, Abingdon, OXON, OX14 4TD, UK. If you have a credit card you may order by telephone – (01253) 831700.

Please enclose a cheque or postal order made payable to Bookpoint Ltd to the value of the cover price and allow the following for postage and packing:
UK & BFPO – £1.00 for the first book, 50p for the second book, and 30p for each additional book ordered up to a maximum charge of £3.00.
OVERSEAS & EIRE – £2.00 for the first book, £1.00 for the second book, and 50p for each additional book.

Name ....

....

Address..

....

If you would prefer to pay by credit card, please complete:
Please debit my Visa/Access/Diner's Card/American Express (delete as applicable) card no:

Signature ....

Expiry Date..

If you would NOT like to receive further information on our products please tick the box. ☐